PRIDE AND THE POOR PRINCESS

The Duke drew Militsa along the passage and as they reached the end of it there was the sound of music.

The Duke had given her his arm, and now as her fingers tightened on his, she said:

"I . . . I shall not know . . . how to . . . behave."

The Duke stopped.

"It is not a party," he answered. "It is in fact a private Chapel. Your father told me to look after you, and that is what I intend to do—as my wife!"

"Y-you are . . . asking me to . . . m-marry you?" She asked in a voice he could barely hear.

"I am not asking you—I am commanding you!"

Then he drew her forward through an open door into the light of the candles on the altar and those flickering in silver sanctuary lamps hanging from the arched roof.

Bantam Books by Barbara Cartland
Ask your bookseller for the titles you have missed

Barbara Cartland's Library of Love Series

Books of Love and Revelation

Other books by Barbara Cartland

Pride
and the
Poor Princess

Barbara Cartland

PRIDE AND THE POOR PRINCESS
A Bantam Book / February 1981

ISBN 0–553–13032–3

Published simultaneously in the United States and Canada

Bantam Books are published by Bantam Books, Inc. Its trade-
mark consisting of the words "Bantam Books" and the por-
trayal of a bantam, is Registered in U.S. Patent and Trademark
Office and in other countries. Marca Registrada. Bantam
Books, Inc., 666 Fifth Avenue, New York, New York 10103.

PRINTED IN THE UNITED STATES OF AMERICA

0 9 8 7 6 5 4 3 2 1

BOOK DESIGNED BY MIERRE

Author's Note

In this novel I have described Constantinople as I found it when I went there in 1928. I had never seen anything so pitiable as the condition of the people in the streets. Snow had fallen and it was terribly cold but a pale sun glittered on the slender minarets and great domes which make the view of the city from the Sea of Marmara one of the most beautiful sights in the world.

But ninety-two percent of the population were illiterate, children walked barefooted, and the mean hovels, squalid dung-hills, crumbling walls, and running sores on emaciated bodies told their own story.

A pathetic attempt was being made to cater for the first trickle of tourists by opening second-rate restaurants and extremely bad cabarets. Champagne was four pounds a bottle and the food was literally poisonous. The waiters and waitresses were white Russians, the remaining dregs of the great influx of refugees who had been able neither to get away to other parts of Europe nor to die.

With their white-stained faces they look pathetically patrician as they hurried to and fro with laden trays which seemed too heavy for them.

When I returned to Turkey in 1970 everything was very different. The city, rechristened Istanbul, was beautiful, prosperous, and comfortable. I was acclaimed the favourite author of the now well-educated Turks, and the only snag during our visit was a minor earthquake!

I am deeply grateful for the facts about the brutal assassination of the Tsar and his family to *The Last of the Romanovs,* written by that brilliant historian and friend of mine, Virginia Cowles

Chapter One

1924

The Duke of Buckminster was sitting in the Saloon of his yacht reading an English newspaper that was nearly a week old.

Sir Harold Nuneaton walked in and looked at him in surprise.

"I thought you were on deck, Buck," he said, "enjoying the beauties of the spires and domes of Constantinople."

"I saw them before the war, Harry," the Duke replied, "and I can't believe they have altered much."

Harry Nuneaton laughed.

"They will be the only thing in Turkey which has not changed," he said. "I hear that Mustafa Kemal has turned the whole place upside down, especially with his insistence on liberating women from the traditional shackles of Islam."

"That will certainly be revolutionary."

The Duke spoke in a somewhat uninterested voice, and Harry Nuneaton crossed the Saloon to sit down beside him in one of the deep, comfortable armchairs which could only have been chosen by a man who appreciated luxury.

"What is the matter, Buck?" he asked. "I thought you have seemed a bit off-colour these last few days."

The Duke did not answer for a moment. Then he threw his *Times* on the floor.

1

"It is nothing serious," he said. "It is just that I am finding life rather dull after all the excitement of the war."

Harry Nuneaton was not surprised.

If anyone had had a glamorous, exciting time during the war it was the Duke.

In charge of an Armoured Car Unit attached to the Royal Naval Air Service, the Duke had been sent to the Western Desert to assist the British Imperial Troops.

His armour-plated Rolls-Royces had taken part in the strangest and most adventurous battles of the war.

They had rescued prisoners who were being starved and ill-treated by one of the enemy Sheiks and they had reinforced small groups who had been detached from the main Armies.

In fact, they had performed such valiant service that Whitehall became deeply interested in what had originally been an experiment of which many Generals had been extremely sceptical.

In fact, they had discovered through the Duke's brilliant leadership that the years he and his officers had spent risking death in motor-cars, motor-boats, and aeroplanes could in an emergency pay amazing dividends in their support of the more-traditional methods of warfare.

"If anyone deserves a decoration for gallantry," a General commanding the Desert Forces had said to Harry Nuneaton after the war, "it is Buckminster. He would never give up; it is not a phrase that exists in his personal vocabulary."

That, Harry Nuneaton knew, was true. At the same time, he realised that while the war had given the Duke an incentive which had previously been lacking in his luxurious life, now that it was ended he was rather like a ship without a rudder.

One of the richest men in England, he had no reason to exert himself except in looking after his huge Estates and producing an heir to carry on the ancient title.

The Dukedom was comparatively new, having

been awarded to his grandfather by Queen Victoria for his services in building up the Empire.

But the Earls of Minster went back to the Sixteenth Century and their family name was interwoven in the history of Great Britain.

What the Duke was finding now, in a mundane world, was that Government was in the hands of small-minded politicians and there was no place for a Duke, however intelligent he might be.

He therefore sank back into the social life that had centred round him before 1914, and he found himself giving the same parties with the same lavishness at the same time of year, for the same reasons as he had done ever since he had inherited the Dukedom at the age of twenty-one.

The only thing that had changed were the women who amused him, because those who had captured his fancy before the war were now too old.

At thirty-five the Duke was finding that even the pretty faces, the tinkling voices, and the inevitable flattery which every woman accorded him could with repetition become boring.

Women were attracted to him not only because of his title.

Well over six feet tall, broad-shouldered and extremely good-looking, he would, his men friends often thought, have been devastating even had he been a nobody.

But with the aura of his wealth and rank he had become a commanding figure who dominated London Society and of course the gossip-columns.

It was understandable that the "Buckminster Set," as it was called, should be of intense interest to those who eagerly opened the more popular newspapers to learn what they were doing day by day.

As Lord Northcliffe had said to his editors:

"Get names into the newspaper, and the more aristocratic the better!"

There was therefore hardly a day when the Duke of Buckminster's name did not appear in the Press, and there were no magazines which did not carry photographs of him.

Looking at him, Harry Nuneaton realised that
the lines of cynicism which had begun to show even
before the war were now becoming more and more
prominent.

There was also a dry, mocking note in his voice,
to be heard not occasionally but almost continually,
and what was to Harry more significant, there was
a hard look in his grey eyes which was very different
from how they had looked during the war.

Although Harry Nuneaton was three years older
than the Duke, he had been with him almost con-
tinuously during the four years of hostilities.

They had suffered the same hardships, the same
unpleasant moments of intense danger, and the same
feelings of horror at the atrocities that had been per-
petrated both by the Germans and by the tribesmen
of the Middle East.

The Turks had also been cruel to their fallen
enemies, which did not surprise him, and because
they had both condemned the way in which they had
treated their prisoners, Harry was surprised that the
Duke was visiting Constantinople while their experiences were still fresh in their memories.

It was in fact Dolly who had been determined
that the yacht should take them up the Sea of
Marmara to what had always been called the "Pearl
of the East."

Harry, who had not been there before, was quite
certain it would prove to be nothing of the sort, but
Dolly had been very determined, and as the Duke
still found her alluring, although Harry fancied he
was beginning to tire a little, she had got her
way.

"Why I really want to visit Constantinople," she
had said frankly, "is to see if I can buy some of the
marvellous Russian sables or, better still, the incredible jewels that I hear those who escaped from
the Bolsheviks have been selling in the Bazaars."

What she meant was that if they were obtainable the Duke would buy them for her, and Harry,
who knew the value of the gems he had already given
her, had asked with a twist of his lips:

"Still collecting, Dolly? I should have thought you might have enough by this time!"

She had not been annoyed at his impertinence but had merely laughed.

"What woman ever has enough jewels?" she enquired. "And as you are aware, Buck can afford it."

Harry had to admit that jewels became her.

She was extremely beautiful in the new modern way that had little in common with the tall Junoesque beauties who had dominated the scene at the beginning of the century.

With her fair fluffy hair, large blue eyes, and perfect pink-and-white complexion, Dolly symbolised the beauty which the men in the trenches had yearned for and prayed that they would remain alive to find when the war was over.

She had a natural gaiety that made everything she said, and did, seem a joke.

Her feet were made for dancing, and her slim body—again, very unlike that of the previous generation—seemed more like a boy's than a girl's.

But she was entirely feminine and had developed the desire and the intention to make a man pay and pay for her favours, being certain in her own mind, although she was too clever to say so, that men appreciated only what was expensive and hard to get.

Having an ambitious mother who had arranged a brilliant marriage for her at eighteen, Dolly at twenty-four as the Countess of Chatham became the leader of a smart young married set which adorned the night-clubs of London and Paris.

When she was clever enough to captivate the attention of the Duke of Buckminster, it was a triumph that vibrated through the dancing-world and made the Dowagers, who still had some sense of propriety, shake their heads.

"Dolly Chatham and Buckminster!" they said disapprovingly to one another. "No good will come of that!"

Six months later they were asking what Robert was doing to allow his wife to get herself talked about in such an outrageous fashion.

The Earl, as it happened, was not particularly interested.

Rather like the Duke, he was finding peace a bore, and the duty of continually squiring a very beautiful wife to parties and night-clubs where she invariably danced with other men was not to his taste.

As he could no longer kill Germans, he had gone out to Africa to shoot big game, and if he was aware of the endless talk and speculation about his wife and the Duke it did not trouble him.

Perhaps it was just a desire for more jewellery that had made Dolly suggest they should go yachting at Easter, or perhaps like Harry she had become aware that Buck was straining a little at the leash and if she wished to keep him she would have to strive to amuse him.

The Duke was quite amenable to leaving London and going in search of the sun.

He also wanted to try out his new yacht, which was the largest in commission since the war and on which he had spent much time not only improving the design but also adding many gadgets of his own invention.

She had been named *The Siren* and there was a great deal of speculation in the Gossip Press as to which particular woman he had in mind.

Whoever she might have been when he first chose the name, there was no doubt that Dolly had appropriated both the title and the position of hostess on this voyage.

She had chosen the other guests with care.

Lord and Lady Radstock were both close friends of the Duke, and Nancy Radstock was Dolly's greatest friend—so far as it was possible for her to have a woman friend at all.

Nancy had the advantage from Dolly's point of view of being no rival when it came to looks, and yet she was always welcomed by the Duke because she was amusing.

She made him laugh, and with her quick wit she prevented there being any awkward moments.

She also unashamedly announced that she wanted to spend as much of her life as possible with the Duke in any part of the world he wished to be, simply because she preferred luxury to the awful effort of keeping up appearances on "poor George's income."

"I am not pretty enough to be a gold-digger," she would say disarmingly, "so I have to be a sponger. You do not mind, do you, Buck dear?"

The Duke would laugh at such honesty and occasionally give her small presents for which she would be effusively grateful, and she was sensible enough not to be jealous of the enormous amount he expended on Dolly.

It was well-known amongst the Duke's friends that he was generous only when it suited him. In other ways he could be quite tight-fisted.

Harry had always thought this was due to his conviction that because he was so wealthy, almost everybody was out to trick him in some way.

It infuriated him that there should be one price for him and another for ordinary people.

Because from an early age he had determined not to be made a fool, he scrutinised every bill and was known to dismiss any employee who attempted in any way, however trivial, to cheat him.

It had been sensible when he first inherited, but now it had become an obsession, and Harry had begun to think that his hardness and cynicism were ruining what was otherwise a very lovable character.

But he was too tactful to say so aloud, and now he had the feeling that the Duke was resenting Dolly's determination to make him pay for more spoils in Constantinople than were really justified by their relationship.

"You cannot put the clock back, Buck," he said aloud, "and I think you will find that when the country has settled down, there will be things to do which you will find interesting."

"It is six years since the war ended," the Duke replied, "and everything still seems chaotic."

"It is bound to be," Harry said. "With a million

men killed and far too many unemployed, our factories out-of-date, and without enough export orders to get production going again, things are bound to be difficult."

"I am fed up with politics," the Duke said in a disagreeable voice.

He felt like this because the politicians would not listen to him and there was no definite part for him to play in the rehabilitation of the country.

Because he wished to change the subject, Harry remarked:

"I shall be interested to see what is happening in Turkey. I have always thought that while it is one thing to dispose of the Sultan, it is another to abolish the office and all that it administered."

The Duke knew that he was speaking sensibly.

Mustafa Kemal, the Military genius who was trying to create the Republic of Turkey, had realised that the Sultanate could not be allowed to continue, but it was going to be difficult to find something to put in its place.

The Sultan himself, in the company of a few eunuchs and personal servants, his jewels packed away in heavy trunks, had slipped out of the Yildiz Kiosk on a bleak November day and boarded a British battleship which had taken him to Malta.

But he had not taken the problems of Turkey with him, and there were still many other drastic changes to be made in the Constitution.

It was something which Harry was longing to talk about, but the Duke was lying back in his chair in a somewhat gloomy silence, and he thought it would be wise to speak of other things.

"By the way," he said, "the Captain tells me he has been warned that we should be careful of what we eat if we go ashore at any port. In fact, it sounds as if we would be wise to stay for meals on the yacht."

"I had no intention of doing anything else!" the Duke snapped. "And if Dolly thinks I am going to trail round that labyrinth of Bazaars, looking for jewels which I very much doubt even exist, she is mistaken!"

"She will be disappointed," Harry said with a smile.

He had the feeling that the Duke shrugged his shoulders, and he thought that Dolly was letting her greed override her better judgement.

He thought that perhaps he should warn her, then wondered why he should bother.

He had seen the Duke pass through many love-affairs and one thing was inevitable: sooner or later they ended, and as soon as one woman slipped out of his life, she was replaced by another.

Then, as if thinking of her made her appear like a genie obeying the call of the master-hand, Dolly came bursting into the Saloon.

She was looking extremely attractive in an expensive fur coat which had been a present from the Duke, with a little hat of the same fur worn over her fair hair, which was fashionably fluffed out at the sides.

Her lips were a provocative crimson, her skin was almost dazzlingly pink and white, and her blue eyes seemed to echo the sky.

"Buck!" she exclaimed, as she entered like a breeze blowing from the snows of Russia. "I have been waiting for you! Do come and look at the city! It is too, too entrancing!"

It was fashionable to talk in an exaggerated manner about everything, and Dolly was the epitome of fashion.

"It is too cold!" the Duke replied. "I cannot think why we did not stay in Monte Carlo—at least it was warmer there."

"But not half so fascinating!" Dolly said. "And I understand we can now visit the Sultan's Palace and even see the Harem!"

She gave a little laugh and sat down on the arm of the Duke's chair to say:

"It is bad luck for you that there are no alluring houris there, but it would be amusing to see where

they once were incarcerated. I wonder what they did
that made them so attractive?"

"There are no prizes for the answer to that question," Harry said with a laugh.

"I am not sure," Dolly said, George has been reading books about Constantinople and he says that every
newcomer to the Harem had to pass through a 'School
of Love' before the Sultan saw her. I want to know
what she learnt."

"I doubt if you would find it very amusing," the
Duke said in a cold voice, "and the penalty for fail-
ure was to have your feet weighed with lead and
to be thrown into the Bosporus by attendants kept
for that special purpose!"

"Is that what you intend to do when you are
bored with me?" Dolly asked. "As I cannot swim,
you would not even have to put weights on my
feet—just push me overboard!"

She spoke as though she expected the Duke to
protest that it was something which would never
happen. Instead he said:

"It is certainly a good way of disposing of things
which are no longer wanted on a voyage!"

"I think you are being beastly to me," Dolly protested, "and I have no wish to stay here talking. I
want to see the minarets and domes, and if you will
not tell me which Mosque they belong to, then I
shall have to find somebody who will!"

Again she spoke provocatively, but the Duke did
not rise to the bait. Instead he said:

"Ask the Captain. He knows these waters well
and is actually a gold-mine of information."

Dolly pouted her red lips.

"You are being a teeny bit disagreeable, my pet,
and I find it too, too damping, so I shall go back on
deck. Come and join us when you feel more cheerful."

As she spoke she put her hand into the Duke's,
but as he did not seem very responsive, she got up
and walked across the Saloon, giving Harry Nuneaton
a dazzling smile as she passed him.

There was no doubt that she was very lovely, but
Harry thought, as he always had done, that there

was something lacking in Dolly; something that made her, despite her looks, a little ordinary when she should have been exceptional.

The Duke picked up the newspaper that was lying beside him on the floor, and because Harry sensed that he wished to be alone, he too left the Saloon and, putting on a heavy overcoat, went on deck.

Dolly, with Nancy and George Radstock, was leaning over the rail looking at the Mosque of Suleiman the Magnificent, with its four pointed minarets silhouetted against the skyline.

It was certainly a very lovely sight, and the waters of the Golden Horn reflected the blue of the sky and shimmered in the sun.

At the same time it was cold, and it was not surprising that Dolly and Nancy were snuggled into their fur coats and occasionally stamped their feet because their ankles in their silk stockings felt the chill wind.

"As soon as we dock I want to go ashore," Dolly said.

"It will be too late by then," George Radstock replied. "You will have to wait until tomorrow. I cannot imagine the Bazaars are very salutary places to be after dark."

"I suppose that is where we will find the jewels," Dolly said.

"If there are any to be had, that is where they will be," George Radstock replied, "but quite frankly, I think we are too late."

"Too late?"

"The Revolution in Russia took place in 1917, seven years ago," George explained, "and although obviously the aristocrats did not all leave at once, those who escaped from the Bolsheviks would, I reckon, have reached Constantinople two or three years later. So their jewels would all have been sold before now."

"You are depressing me!" Dolly said crossly. "Several people in London told me that they had recently seen fantastic necklaces, tiaras, and brooches for sale if only they had had enough money to buy them."

"Well, if Buck is willing, that will not happen to you," Harry said a little sarcastically.

"Of course he will buy me what I want," Dolly replied quickly—a little too quickly, Harry thought.

"Be sure he buys the genuine article," Harry cautioned. "Buck dislikes being taken for a mug."

Dolly looked at him wide-eyed.

"Are you suggesting there might be imitations for sale?"

"Why not? The Oriental craftsmen are very clever fellows. If they can palm you off with an emerald which is only a bit of green glass or a diamond which is really crystal, they will do so."

"We must be careful, very, very careful." Dolly said with a note of concern in her voice. "Nothing would upset Buck more than if he was deceived by a fake!"

"If you take my advice," Harry said, "you will go to a reputable jeweller. You may have to pay a bit more, but at least you would know you were getting the genuine article."

Dolly gave a cry.

"But that would not be half as much fun as finding a real bargain, which had once belonged to a Russian aristocrat, at some cheap stall where the seller has no idea of its value."

"What you are really saying," Harry said sharply, "is that you are trying to find jewellery that has been stolen from some wretched woman who has been fleeing for her life and has had to sell it at a knock-down price to save herself from starvation."

He spoke scathingly and Nancy Radstock gave a little cry of horror.

"Who wants to buy anything like that? I am sure it would be unlucky. They say jewels can portray the emotions of those who wear them, and I would never, never want to wear anything which might bring me bad luck!"

"Nonsense!" Dolly said sharply. "Harry is only trying to frighten us. Personally, diamonds, pearls, and emeralds have always brought me good luck, if only for the reason that Buck is ready to give them to me!"

"As you say, you are very, very lucky to have him," Nancy said, "so do not risk it all by buying anything which might have an evil influence on you."

"You are jealous, that's what is wrong with all of you," Dolly declared. "Whatever you may say, I shall go looking for treasures in the Bazaars, and when I find them you will all have to eat your words!"

As Harry had anticipated, by the time they docked it was far too late for anyone to go ashore, and Dolly wanted to play Mah-jong.

When the Duke refused to join the game, Harry sat down at the table knowing that Dolly would insist on playing for higher stakes than either he or George could afford.

The Duke went to the cabin that was his own special sanctum, where he could escape from his guests and be alone.

The Siren was so large and so well planned that the party could have been far larger had not Dolly been determined to keep it intimate.

Now the Duke thought it was a mistake that they were so few. He wanted to talk to Harry, but that would have meant the others could not play Mah-jong.

However, there were more newspapers which he had not yet read, and he sat down in one of the red leather armchairs in the cabin.

He switched on the reading-lamp that he had designed himself so that it remained at exactly the right angle however rough the sea might be.

He had just turned to the Editorial in the *Morning Post* when a steward came into the cabin.

"Excuse me, Your Grace. There's a woman here who says she's got a letter which she'll only give personally into Your Grace's own hands."

The Duke looked up in surprise.

"Why did she say that?"

"I don't know, Your Grace, but she refused to hand the letter over to anyone else, and also says she won't go away 'til Your Grace has received it."

"Is this a method of begging?" the Duke enquired.

"I don't know, Your Grace. But I've been warned and warned what the beggars are like here."

He paused for a moment before he added:

"The woman speaks with an educated voice, Your Grace, but she's poorly dressed, and from what I've seen she could do with a square meal."

The Duke was interested.

"You say she definitely will not give the letter to anyone except myself?"

"She's been arguing with me, Your Grace, for nigh on fifteen minutes. I tells her in our country we has servants to carry things like letters to the Master. But her sticks to her guns, so to speak, and nothing I can say'll move her!"

The steward, who had been in his service for a long time, spoke in such an aggrieved fashion that the Duke laughed.

"Very well, Stevens. Bring the woman down, and take care she doesn't steal anything on the way!"

"You can be sure of that, Your Grace!"

Stevens left him, and the Duke, with a faint smile on his lips, put down his newspaper and rose to sit at his flat-topped desk which stood at one end of the cabin.

He thought that perhaps he was making a mistake in allowing the woman to come aboard. At the same time, he was curious to see what the letter contained.

'It is probably an invitation to visit some Restaurant or night-club,' he thought, 'or perhaps merely an advertising gimmick on the part of some shop.'

Then he told himself that in that case it would be unlikely they would send somebody poorly dressed, and certainly not a woman.

Despite the talk of liberating women, Turkey was still completely a man's world; and the Ottoman defeat in the war, which might have humiliated the soldiers as fighters, had definitely not made them any less aggressive as men.

The Duke waited. Then he heard footsteps outside and the door opened.

"The woman, Your Grace!" the steward announced.

The Duke looked up expectantly.

The woman who came into the cabin was certainly poorly dressed.

She was wearing the thick shapeless garment of a peasant, the skirt reaching almost to the ground, and covering her head was a wide woollen scarf of a nebulous hue with the ends drawn back over her shoulders.

Because it was growing dusk and the Duke had not put on the other lights in the cabin, it was difficult to see her face since the scarf was pulled well forward.

She did not speak but moved towards the desk and held out a letter in a white envelope.

The Duke took it from her.

"Thank you," he said. "I understand you speak English?"

"Yes, Your Grace."

The voice was low and he thought musical.

"I hear you would not leave this letter with my servants. Have you any particular reason for refusing to do so?"

"It is from someone you once knew, Your Grace, and is written to you in confidence. You will understand the need for secrecy when you read it."

The woman was obviously well educated, the Duke decided. Her English was almost perfect, and she spoke with only a slight, rather attractive accent.

At the same time, the manner in which she spoke had a cool impersonality about it which struck him as strange.

He had somehow expected her to be eager and subservient, but she was neither of those things.

He had a feeling that she was standing apart, almost divorced in some strange manner from what was taking place round her.

He looked at her searchingly and thought that she seemed extremely thin, and he saw that the hand which held the letter was blue-veined and with the wrist-bone sharply protruding.

Also, the skin was very white, which told him that she certainly was not Turkish.

A sudden thought struck him and he said:

"Will you sit down while I read this letter, and perhaps accept some refreshment?"

"It is unnecessary, Your Grace. I am only the messenger who has conveyed the letter to you in safety."

However, the Duke rose and walked across the cabin.

There was as usual an open bottle of champagne in an ice-cooler which was placed there after tea was finished in case he or any of his male guests should want a drink.

With the wine Stevens always put out a selection of salted nuts, olives, and a plate of small, thinly cut pâté sandwiches.

The Duke picked up the plate of sandwiches and carried it to where the woman was sitting.

"I am sure you will join me in a glass of champagne," he said, "and let me offer you a sandwich."

For a moment he thought she was going to refuse. Then with an inarticulate murmur she took one of the sandwiches from the plate, but slowly, so slowly that he was almost sure she was controlling an impulse to move quicker.

He put the plate down beside her on the corner of his desk, poured out two glasses of champagne, and carried them across the cabin; he put one on his desk beside the plate of sandwiches and carried the other to where he sat down opposite her.

He glanced at the woman as he did so and saw that she was eating the sandwich slowly, taking such small bites that he was sure she was deliberately making it last as long as possible.

He remembered seeing men he had rescued in the desert, who had been starved by their captors almost to the point of death, eating in very much the same way.

One had always expected them to gobble. In-

stead, as if when they did have food it was so precious, they savoured every morsel.

Picking up a gold letter-opener, the Duke slit
the envelope, pulled out the piece of writing-paper,
and read it.

It did not take long, for the letter was short.
Then he said to the woman opposite him:

"Do you know what this letter contains?"

"Yes, Your Grace."

"I remember Prince Ivan Kerenski. As he says,
we met in St. Petersburg when I was there in 1913."

The woman did not speak, but the Duke fancied
that her eyes in the shadows were looking at him
intently.

"The Prince tells me that he has a treasure of
importance that he thinks I will find interesting, and
I see I have to be guided by you to where it is hidden. Is that correct?"

"Yes."

The answer was no more than a monosyllable.

"Are you suggesting that it would be dangerous
for the Prince to come to me?"

The woman inclined her head slowly.

"But why? I cannot understand. Surely if he has
reached Constantinople he can no longer be in any
danger from the Bolsheviks?"

There was silence for a moment. Then the
woman said:

"The Prince will explain to you what the position is."

The Duke again looked down at the letter.

He had never seen the Prince's handwriting, but
there was no doubt that the letter was written in a
cultured hand and the phrasing was what one would
expect from the type of Russian aristocrat that he
knew the Prince to be.

He remembered him well.

He had been staying in St. Petersburg as the
guest of the Tsar and Tsarina, and Prince Ivan had
been one of the noblemen constantly in attendance.

The Duke recalled meeting him every day at
some entertainment or another.

Thinking back, it now seemed a background of incredible luxury, of gold and malachite pillars, of priceless paintings, of servants so numerous that they fell over themselves in their efforts to supply every comfort a guest could require.

Also, there had been the company of exquisite women glittering with jewels as the men glittered with elaborate decorations.

It was almost impossible to think that in so short a space of time all that had vanished—the Tsar and Tsarina and their children had been shot, the aristocrats who surrounded them had been executed, while a few, and apparently amongst them Prince Ivan, still faced dangers.

The Duke put the letter down on his desk.

"I will of course be delighted to meet Prince Ivan as he suggests. Perhaps you will explain to me what you want me to do."

"You are to come alone or with one other person," the woman replied. "No-one must know where you are going, and it is imperative you should not mention the Prince's name to anybody, not even to your guests."

For the first time since she had begun speaking to him, the intonation in the woman's voice changed from an impersonal and aloof note to one which undoubtedly held a tremor of fear.

"You must leave after dark," she went on. "I will be waiting for you at the end of the Quay in an ordinary hired carriage. Please step into it quickly. Ask no questions and do not speak to the driver."

There was a faintly cynical smile on the Duke's lips as he asked:

"Is this 'cloak-and-dagger' business really necessary?"

"I assure Your Grace," the woman replied, "that not only the Prince's life but other people's lives are dependent upon the utmost secrecy."

She certainly spoke seriously and with a sincerity that was impressive.

"Very well," the Duke said. "I will do as you say."

He glanced at the port-hole and realised that although it was not quite six o'clock, it was already dark.

"Would this time tomorrow suit you?" he asked.

"Yes, Your Grace."

"I will go to the end of the Quay as you suggest," the Duke said, "and I will bring with me just one man. His name is Sir Harold Nuneaton. The Prince may have met him when he was in London."

The woman did not seem interested, and the Duke said:

"If that is all, I suggest you drink some of your champagne and please have another sandwich."

He was convinced by now that she was hungry. Why he should be so sure of it, he was not certain. He just knew that the impression was there.

Once again she took a sandwich, holding it delicately between her thumb and first finger.

The Duke thought he should keep her company and he rose to his feet to fetch the small silver dishes containing nuts and olives from a table in the corner of the cabin.

He picked them up, and as he turned he saw her move her hand slightly and was certain that she had seized the opportunity of taking another sandwich and concealing it in the pocket of her coat.

He wondered if it was for Prince Ivan and what she meant in his life, but he merely carried the silver dishes back to the desk and placed them down in front of her.

"Now tell me about yourself," he said. "Are you Russian like the Prince?"

He was quite sure she was, but he wanted her to confirm it.

"I am not important, Your Grace," she answered, "and now I think I should leave. If anyone asks why I called to see you, would you say that I was asking if you had any orders for fresh flowers from the Bazaar?"

"I think it unlikely that I should be questioned," the Duke said a little drily, "but of course I am prepared to give that answer should it happen."

"Thank you."

The woman rose to her feet and he noticed that she had barely touched her glass of champagne and only two sandwiches had been taken from the plate.

The Duke opened the door of the cabin and she moved out in an imperious way which told him it was second nature to her to have doors opened for her to pass through them first.

It was something he had not expected, from her appearance, and yet as she walked ahead of him he was certain that he was right. She was in herself very different from what she looked.

They reached the door which opened onto the deck and she stopped.

"Please do not come any farther, Your Grace," she said. "I must not be seen talking to you."

She did not wait for the Duke to reply, but slipped through the door and out into the darkness.

The Duke was intrigued. He wondered if there was anyone waiting for her on the Quay and wanted to go out on deck to see her walk away.

Then he told himself that if there was really any danger, he might be making things difficult for her and perhaps it would be impossible for her to be waiting for him tomorrow as she had arranged.

Because he could think of nothing more annoying than to go through the rest of his life being curious as to what Prince Ivan wished to tell him, he stayed where he was.

"I must play this woman's game by her rules," he told himself.

He waited for a few moments, then walked towards the Saloon.

His guests had obviously just finished their game and Harry had risen to his feet to stretch his legs.

"Come on, Buck," he said as the Duke entered. "You can take my place. Dolly has all the luck and I really cannot afford to play against her."

"I want to talk to you, Harry," the Duke said.

There was a note in his voice which made his friend look at him sharply.

"Oh no!" Dolly protested. "I want you to dance

with me. I will not allow you to go off gossiping with Harry in your sanctum from which we women are so frequently barred! Come and dance to just one record. Then it will be time to dress for dinner."

She put a record on the Gramophone as she spoke.

"I want to talk to Harry," the Duke argued. "It is important."

"More important than I?" Dolly asked.

She spoke as if such an idea was preposterous.

"Actually, the answer to that is 'yes,'" the Duke said.

Without waiting for her reply, he went from the Saloon as he spoke, and Harry followed him.

Dolly stared after them at first in surprise, then with a frown between her blue eyes. She slammed the lid of the Gramophone down in a temper.

Chapter Two

The open carriage in which they were travelling carried them across the Galata Bridge, which had been built by the Germans in 1913 to replace an old wooden structure.

Beneath it on the Golden Horn plied the big ferry-boats and smaller craft of every kind.

What the Duke knew, since he had been in Constantinople before, was that under the iron arches were stalls of every sort and description, besides boot-blacks and newspaper boys, beggars, and piles of fish which had just been caught in the sea.

Dolly, however, was interested only in reaching the Bazaar.

She had searched in an ancient guide-book for descriptions of the labyrinth in which there was a maze of small shops, grouped by traders who, she was told, sold everything from spices to jewels, from mandrake roots to leeches.

When they reached it, it was to find that the Bazaar was covered over, which gave the place a strange and mystic atmosphere, redolent with the spices which were everywhere in huge baskets and sacks.

Harry found this rather interesting, having never been to a Spice Market before. But Dolly hurried them all on, talking only to the guide who had ar-rived at the yacht with the carriage and apparently understood her instructions that she wished to see jewels.

The Duke, Harry thought, was in a particularly good humour this morning, and he thought it must be due to the new interest which had been given him the previous evening.

When he took Harry down to his cabin and told him what had occurred, he had in fact been somewhat suspicious.

"Do you really believe that a Prince, who you tell me was of great importance in St. Petersburg, is really hiding here in Constantinople?"

"Read the letter yourself," the Duke replied. "And while I have not seen Prince Ivan's handwriting, I am quite certain this was written by a cultured man."

Harry inspected the letter and was forced to admit that the Duke was right.

"What was the woman like?"

"It was difficult to see her," the Duke replied. "Her face was in shadow, but she was obviously well educated and her English was almost perfect."

He told Harry about the sandwiches.

"I thought, when I saw a movement," he said, "that she was taking one from the plate to take back to the Prince, but she may in fact have been concealing it for herself."

"You might have offered her the rest," Harry suggested.

The Duke shook his head.

"No, I suspect she is an aristocrat and they are incredibly, unbelievably proud. I remember when I was in St. Petersburg thinking they were the proudest people in the world. They would never become the sort of poverty-stricken beggars you can tip."

"The Prince is obviously prepared to accept your money," Harry said.

"Judging by this letter, he intends to sell me something, which is a very different matter," the Duke retorted. "And I do not mind betting you, Harry, however hard up he may be, if I offered him money for nothing he would not take it."

He thought that Harry was looking sceptical, and he added:

"You do not know the Russians as I do. They are a strange people, and the sufferings of those who have not been killed by the Bolsheviks must be terrible in a world where nobody wants them."

Harry looked at him in surprise.

It was unlike the Duke to be compassionate or even sympathetic with the under-dog, but he said nothing, and only hoped that this new diversion would be as interesting tomorrow as it appeared to be today.

The Bazaar was crowded, but it seemed that no-one was buying from the stalls and small shops, which had pitifully little to offer.

The Duke had noticed as they drove through the streets that the people, moving slowly over the dirty, broken pavements, looked half-starved.

There were children walking barefoot and now a woman came up to them holding out for alms a skeleton-like hand with hennaed nails, while the baby she carried looked too frail to live more than a few hours.

The Duke gave her some coins and she hurried away as if he might repent his generosity and ask for them back.

Dolly was still forging ahead, her rich fur coat looking very out-of-place amongst the rags and shapeless garments worn by other passers-by.

Many of the Turkish women still wore veils and the enveloping black burnous.

Despite the voluminous folds, the women gave the impression of being slim and hungry beneath them.

Dolly stopped when the guide brought her to a small shop where a few cheap watches were displayed and there was also a basin of small coins from foreign countries.

Dolly looked at them with an expression of contempt, then went inside with the guide.

He explained volubly and with extravagant gestures of his hands what the lady required.

The shop-keeper, an old man who looked cold and miserable, only shrugged his shoulders.

He gave a curt reply and the guide said to Dolly:

"He say lady come too late. Two—three years ago, good jewels very cheap. Now all gone!"

"Where have they gone?" Dolly persisted.

There was a long interchange of words, from which transpired the information that jewel-buyers from overseas had bought up everything that was available.

The Duke, listening from the doorway, knew this was what he had expected, but Dolly was not yet defeated.

"What about furs?" she asked the guide. "Russian sables? Surely they are obtainable somewhere in Constantinople?"

The guide said there was a place he knew where they might have some furs for sale, but he was not sure.

"Take us there!" Dolly commanded.

They walked back again towards the great door of the Bazaar.

"I want to see the Palace," Nancy announced.

She and her husband had been wandering round on their own, looking at the spices and at the other shops and stalls.

Now she came to the Duke's side to say:

"I think these people are terribly sad! They have nothing to sell, and yet they still must eat. What will become of them?"

"I imagine a more stable Government will do something about food eventually," the Duke said in a not-very-hopeful tone.

"In the meantime, what about the children?" Nancy asked beneath her breath.

Then, as there was nothing for them in the Bazaar, they followed Dolly out into the sunshine.

A clear sun glittered on the slender minarets and the great domes. The city was very beautiful, but it was difficult not to think how superficial it was, when there was so much ugliness and poverty in the streets.

They drove a long way down narrow, cobbled

lanes with houses on either side of them which were black with age and neglect.

The guide stopped the carriage in a dirty yard and went inside a tall house which had most of the glass in its windows broken.

He was away for some time and the Duke said:

"I have a feeling this is going to be a very cheap day as far as I am concerned."

"I am sure they really have things hidden away somewhere," Dolly insisted, "if we could only find them."

She slipped her hand into the Duke's.

"Help me, Buck!" she pleaded. "You know how clever you are at finding things, and I do so want a souvenir of Constantinople."

"I cannot buy you what is unobtainable," he replied.

"You speak to the man. Tell him that you can afford to pay a lot of money for something that is really valuable."

"If he had anything of value," the Duke said, "he would have produced it by now, you may be sure of that!"

As he spoke, the guide returned to the side of the carriage, bringing with him an aged hunchback wearing an old shawl round his shoulders to keep out the cold.

"This man say," the guide explained, "he find lady some furs by tonight. He get bear or goat, but nothing else."

"Of course I do not want such rubbish!" Dolly said sharply. "There must be sables somewhere in the place when we are so near to Russia!"

The guide translated this to the hunchback, who merely repeated what the jeweller had said—that any sables there had been in Constantinople had been bought up several years ago.

"You win!" Dolly said to the Duke. "But I cannot pretend I am not disappointed."

She spoke as if it were his fault, and Harry wondered if she might not have a surprise later if

Prince Ivan could produce a treasure that was really worth buying.

Thinking that Dolly was likely to make everybody depressed because she had not got what she wanted, he suggested that they should go and find a place where they could have something to drink.

"We mustn't eat anything," he said, "but there must be a Restaurant where we can have some coffee or perhaps even a bottle of Turkish wine."

"Oh, please let us see the Seraglio first!" Nancy begged. "It cannot be far from here."

They found that the Topkapi Saray was in fact only five minutes' drive away, and they set off, the guide rattling information at them parrot-fashion.

Dolly cheered up when she saw the huge wall of the Palace with its towers and impressive entrance.

"Now we shall see the Harem," she said.

The guide, sitting on the box above their heads, heard what she said and bent backwards to say:

"Lady see Sultan's jewels."

Dolly's eyes glittered.

"That's what I want!" she exclaimed.

They alighted from the carriage and walked towards the great gate.

"Now for ghosts of eunuchs, odalisques, catamite pages, drunken Viziers, and depraved Sultans," Harry teased.

The Duke was not listening. He was thinking that the Palace, built by Sultan Mehemet, had been like a town whose inhabitants at one time had numbered five thousand.

It had been not only the official residence of the Sultan but also the seat of Government of the Empire.

The guide took them into a courtyard.

He informed them that the first gate was called: "Bab-I-Humayun," the Gate of Felicity, on which had been exhibited the heads of decapitated officials.

The next gate, he said with glee, was the Gate of Peace, and beside it was the executioner's block and the tap where he afterwards washed his hands.

To pass through the Gate of Happiness, he continued, meant instant death!

Everything was empty, dusty, and depressing, until on Dolly's insistence the guide took them to a third courtyard, where the treasures left behind by the Sultan were being assembled to form a Museum.

This was what Dolly had been wanting to see, and she stood staring open-mouthed at the eighty-six-carat Spoon Diamond, and the rubies, pearls, diamond-studded coffee cups, and emeralds four inches square.

The emeralds were certainly fantastic, but the Duke and Harry were looking at one of the most notable relics of Constantinople, which was reputed to be the right arm of St. John the Baptist.

Dolly slipped her arm through the Duke's.

"Come and look at these emeralds, Buck," she begged. "They are what I hoped to find. This is what I want."

"I doubt if they would entertain an offer, however large, for the Sultan's sword or for the emeralds he wore in his turban," the Duke replied drily.

"What is the use of them just stuck here with no-one to look at them?"

"They will attract tourists," Harry said, "and I am quite certain that Mustafa Kemal has already thought that they will bring in the foreign currency which he certainly needs at the moment."

Dolly was not listening and took only a perfunctory look at the other parts of the Palace.

She was soon amenable to Harry's suggestion that they should now go and find something to drink.

The guide took them to a Restaurant that was poor and obviously in need of decoration, but he informed them that it was the best available.

They sat down and the Duke was instantly aware that the waiters were not Turkish and were obviously of a very different class from the other customers.

They hurried to and fro laden with trays of food, while the people they served kept complaining about both the service and what they ate.

Nancy was watching them too and she said in a low voice to the Duke:

"I feel it is a matter of life and death for them to keep their jobs."

"I was thinking the same thing," he replied.

As he spoke, a young waiter dropped a banana from a bowl of fruit.

A look of absolute terror came over his face, and another waiter quickly covered the banana with a napkin and carried it out of sight, just as round a large screen that shut off the kitchen from the Restaurant came the Proprietor.

He was a huge, heavy-bellied Turk with a sharpness in his dark eyes which boded ill for anyone who offended him.

The Duke had ordered some coffee and a bottle of wine and when they came they were both undrinkable.

Harry, looking at what the other people in the Restaurant were having, said:

"You know what we ought to have ordered?"

"What is that?" Nancy enquired.

"It is a sherbet which is, I read somewhere, a peculiar drink made by the Turks."

"What does it contain?" Nancy asked.

"Lemon, sugar, amber, and a number of other ingredients, but I doubt if we would find it very palatable."

"I personally have no intention of trying it," the Duke said firmly. "Let us go back to the yacht. We were warned not to eat or drink in Constantinople, so we will have no excuse if we make ourselves ill."

As he spoke, his eyes met Harry's and they were both thinking that it was important they should be well for tonight.

There were no protests about leaving from either Dolly or Nancy, and as they drove back, there was a general silence as if all they had seen had depressed them.

Yet as they drove beside the glittering water of the Golden Horn and saw everywhere the thin elegant minarets silhouetted against the blue sky, it

seemed wrong that there should be such a contrast
between the beauty of the "Pearl of the East" and
the human beings who had to live in it.

"Perhaps things will get better in the future,"
Nancy said hopefully as they went aboard the yacht.

"They can hardly get worse!" the Duke remarked.

They had luncheon late and there seemed to be
no point in doing any further sight-seeing.

They played cards for a short while, and after
tea the Duke said that he had some work to do and
did not wish to be disturbed.

"Do I disturb you?" Dolly asked with a carress-
ing note in her voice. "That is what I want to do!"

The Duke did not answer and she went on:

"If you want to be alone I will go and lie down
and read a book. I have an exciting new novel by
Michael Arlen which I brought with me."

"Lend it to me after you have finished with it,"
Nancy said. "I adore the way he writes!"

They went to their cabins, and as George followed his wife, the Duke was left alone with Harry.

"What is the time?" he asked. "We do not wish
to leave too soon and make ourselves conspicuous."

"It is quarter-to-six," Harry replied. "And if you
do not want to be noticed, I think you should wear
a dark overcoat."

He looked down at the Duke's white yachting-
trousers as he spoke.

"I have every intention of doing that," he replied, "and we shall certainly need overcoats. When
the sun goes down it is going to be very cold, if it
does not snow."

He spoke conventionally enough, but Harry knew
from the note in his voice that he was anticipating
an adventure and was therefore no longer bored as
he had been yesterday before he had received the
letter from the Prince.

"I hope we are not going to be disappointed,"
Harry said, "and find this is just a trick to extract
money from you for some jewellery that is not worth
sixpence."

"I shall be surprised if Prince Ivan does not give

us value for our money," the Duke answered. "Incidentally, in case we are being taken for a ride, I do not intend to carry too much money on me."

"That is certainly a wise precaution," Harry approved.

They waited until it was about three minutes to six, then wearing their overcoats they sauntered on deck.

There was one of the Duke's crew on duty near the gangway and as they passed the man the Duke said:

"Sir Harold and I are going for a walk. If anybody asks for me, say I shall be back in an hour."

"Very good, Your Grace," the man replied.

They stepped onto the Quay, which appeared to be deserted.

As they walked over the slush-covered cobbles, Harry wondered if in fact someone was watching and they were being spied upon.

They reached the end of the Quay and for a moment the Duke thought that there was no carriage there to meet them and the woman had not kept her word.

Then he saw a vehicle on the other side of the road. Harry saw it at the same time, and without speaking they moved towards it.

It was a very ancient covered carriage drawn by a thin horse whose bones were showing. The coachman was crouched on the box as if he was half-asleep and not particularly interested whether he had a fare or not.

Then as they reached the side of the carriage the door opened although there was no sign of anyone.

The Duke stepped forward to look into the darkness inside, and as he did so a voice said sharply:

"Quickly! Get in quickly!"

It was a command. The Duke obeyed, followed by Harry, who shut the carriage door behind him.

Immediately the horse moved off.

"Were you followed?"

The woman asked the question in a low voice, as if she was afraid she might be overheard.

"I do not think so," the Duke replied. "There appeared to be no-one about."

The woman turned round to kneel on the seat and look out the small window in the back of the hood.

The glass in it was cracked in several places but she could still see through it, and a few seconds passed before she gave what sounded like a sigh of relief and sat down again.

As she did so, the Duke said:

"I think I should introduce my friend, Sir Harold Nuneaton. I realised yesterday after you had left that you had not told me your name."

"It is not important at the moment," the woman said in the same cold, impersonal voice he remembered.

"Would you care to tell me where we are going?" the Duke asked.

"That too is unnecessary," she replied. "If Your Grace will wait patiently, everything will be explained to you later."

The way she spoke, even more than what she said told the Duke that she had no wish to talk to him, and he therefore made himself as comfortable as he could in the corner of the badly upholstered, inadequately sprung carriage and lapsed into silence.

He wondered what Harry, who was sitting opposite him on the small seat, was thinking.

He was quite certain that he was trying to peer through the darkness inside the carriage to see what their companion looked like.

The lights in the streets through which they passed were very inadequate, and although they drove over the Galata Bridge, the Duke was not able to identify any other landmarks outside or to see their companion inside.

Although she did not speak, he was vividly conscious of her in a way that surprised him.

It was almost as if he could feel vibrations coming from her, and with a perception that was unusual he knew that they were hostile to him personally.

It was all very strange.

At the same time, he felt for the moment as if he were back in the war, fighting against an enemy in a superior position and knowing that every moment might be his last on earth.

They drove for perhaps twenty-five minutes, and then as the carriage began to slow down the woman spoke.

"If you will stay here for a moment," she said, "I will get out and see if there is anyone about. If there is not, I will go ahead and open the door of the house for you. Move as swiftly as you can down the short path. It would be a mistake to linger or to look round you."

She did not wait for a reply, for at that moment the carriage came to a halt. She opened the door and got out.

Through the dirty window they could see her glance right and left, then walk straight ahead.

"Follow her" the Duke said. "God knows what we are letting ourselves in for!"

"I must admit I feel rather apprehensive," Harry replied.

Then they were walking up a small covered path as the woman had told them to do and they heard the carriage drive away.

It struck the Duke suddenly that it might be difficult to get back to the yacht, but there was nothing he could do but pass through a narrow entrance to find the woman waiting for them.

She closed the door and they were in complete darkness.

"Stay where you are!" she commanded. "When I open the door ahead there will be enough light for you to see your way."

She moved away from them as she spoke, and a few seconds later there was just a faint light which showed them in which direction to walk.

The Duke went first, and he found himself in a room that was obviously at the back of a house. To his surprise, it was lit by two candles standing on the floor.

The room was completely unfurnished save for two wooden boxes on which, apparently as a concession to comfort, there were two rough sacks.

The walls were peeling and the windows of the room were boarded up.

The Duke looked round him enquiringly, then glanced at the woman.

"Please sit down," she said. "I will tell the Prince you are here."

There was another door at the far end and she went through it, closing it behind her.

Because she had asked him to do so, the Duke sat down on one of the wooden boxes and Harry sat on the other.

"What do you think all this means?" Harry asked in a low voice.

"God knows," the Duke replied.

"I think this is an empty house," Harry said in a voice barely above a whisper.

"That is obvious," the Duke agreed.

The door through which the woman had left now opened and two men came into the room.

The Duke looked at the newcomers with an expression of incredulity.

Both were heavily bearded and wearing the ragged, dirty garments of the beggers they had seen in the streets.

It flashed through the Duke's mind that they had been tricked and trapped. Then the first man spoke.

"Good-evening, Your Grace!"

The Duke stared at him.

"Can you be . . . ?"

"Yes, I am Ivan Kerenski."

The Duke would have risen to his feet, but to his astonishment the Prince drew a revolver from his tattered garments and pointed it at him.

"I have asked Your Grace here," he said harshly, "so that I can demand from you the assistance I need, which I have no other way of obtaining."

"Demand?" the Duke questioned. "Is there any reason why anything that you wish to ask of me cannot be asked in a reasonable and civilised manner?"

"I doubt if you would listen to me under different circumstances," the Prince replied, and there was an unmistakably bitter note in his voice.

"I certainly have no alternative at the moment but to hear what you have to say," the Duke said.

He spoke coldly and calmly, but he was considerably surprised not only by the Prince's behaviour but by his appearance.

Could it be possible that this was the suave, elegant, handsome man, diplomatic to his finger-tips, whom he had known and liked in St. Petersburg?

The Prince, still holding his revolver, moved a little nearer to the Duke, while the man who was with him, and who looked no less disreputable, stayed where he was just inside the door, and the woman stood beside him.

"What we are demanding of you, Your Grace," the Prince said, "is that you convey the treasure which I mentioned in my letter, and us, in your yacht to Cairo. It is our only possible means of escape, and as we are on the verge of starvation we have no other method of achieving our survival except by threatening you into doing what we want."

"And what is this treasure?" the Duke enquired.

For a moment the Prince did not reply, and the Duke knew that he was debating whether to tell him the truth or to lie.

Then he said:

"The treasure we have hidden here, and for whom we demand you help, is the Grand Duke Alexis!"

If he had intended to startle the Duke he succeeded.

"The Grand Duke Alexis!" he exclaimed. "But he was reported to have been executed by the Bolsheviks."

"That is what they intended," the Prince said grimly, "and that is what they have been trying to do ever since the Revolution began."

"You mean that you have managed to keep His Royal Highness safe all these years?"

Prince Ivan nodded.

"We were helped by the fact that the Grand Duke

was not in St. Petersburg when the Revolution started, but was on his way South. It was some time before we learnt that the Bolsheviks had assumed power and were determined to kill all the Royal Family."

He paused before he went on in a voice that seemed raw:

"It was only when our friends brought us the news that the Tsar and Tsarina had been assassinated, and that the Grand Duke was also reported dead, that we realised the danger he was in."

"I can understand your predicament," the Duke murmured.

"We took the Grand Duke into hiding," the Prince went on, "and by 'we' I mean his Nephew Prince Alexander Saronov."

He indicated the other man with his hand before he added:

"And his daughter, Her Serene Highness Princess Militsa."

The Duke glanced for a moment at the woman standing in the background. The light from the candles barely reached her and he thought she looked as anonymous and enigmatic as she had when she had come to the yacht last night.

Then his eyes went back to Prince Ivan, who continued:

"We have moved month after month, year after year, along the coast of the Black Sea, waiting for an opportunity to escape from Russia."

His voice deepened when he said:

"Yet we were afraid to leave our own people, who, because they had no liking for the Revolutionaries, were prepared to give us enough food to keep us alive, if nothing else."

He looked at Prince Alexander as if he wished to feel sure he agreed with what he was saying, then went on:

"A month ago we learnt that the Bolshevik agents were on our tail, and we managed to find a ship to bring us to Constantinople. It cost us the last roubles we had left in our possession."

"And now you want to reach Cairo?" the Duke said, as the Prince finished speaking.

"I have a little money in a Bank there," the Prince answered, "and I also have friends who might help me find employment of some sort, while Alexander is determined to join the Foreign Legion."

"It sounds a reasonable request," the Duke said, "and you could have asked me to take you without threatening me with a gun."

"And have you go back on your word like your King did?" the Prince snapped.

The way he spoke told the Duke how bitterly he resented how King George V had at first promised the Imperial Family asylum in England after the Revolution had started, then had changed his mind.

It had been agreed at a Cabinet Meeting that an invitation should be sent to the Tsar and Tsarina and their children to come to England.

They had asked if they could join their cousins King George and Queen Mary, and for two-and-a-half years of war Russia had proved herself a dependable ally.

No sooner had the invitation been sent than King George V began to regret it.

His secretary, Lord Stamfordham, wrote to the Russian Foreign Secretary telling him of the King's concern about the remarks that Labour Members of Parliament were making in the House of Commons.

The King began to wonder if a different plan could not be made, and a few days later the Russian Foreign Secretary was informed that opposition to the Emperor and Empress of Russia coming to England was so strong that the invitation was withdrawn.

The Duke, like many other aristocrats at the time, thought it extremely shabby behaviour on the part of the English which would be deeply resented by those Russian aristocrats who were still alive.

"No," Prince Ivan was saying now, "I cannot trust you, after saying that you will help us, not to decide when you are safely back in your yacht that you have no wish to be involved, and leave us to our fate."

"If you will not accept my word that I am willing to help you," the Duke said, "what other method do you suggest?"

"The Princess," Prince Ivan replied, "who has seen your yacht, has suggested that I must keep you here as a prisoner until the Grand Duke is safely aboard, at which time we will release you. And make no mistake, my revolver will be pointed at your heart until the yacht is out of Turkish waters."

"A very clever idea!" the Duke conceded. "At the same time, if you are being followed, as you say, is it not reasonable to think that the Bolshevik agents, if they are watching the yacht, will notice a number of strangers who are not particularly well dressed going aboard?"

There was silence, and as the Duke saw that the Prince was seeing the common sense of this argument, he continued:

"There will also be a definite interval while my letter, which I imagine you intend to force me to write, is taken to the Captain, and any Bolshevik gunman would be able to pick off his victims one by one as they stand on deck."

The Prince gave a little sigh and lowered his revolver.

He looked at the Princess and said:

"I told you it was a hopeless idea. What does it really matter if they shoot us down here or on the Quay? We are still caught like rats in a trap!"

She made a little sound that was a stifled cry before the Duke said:

"Now you listen to me!"

The Russians turned their faces towards him and he knew that he held their attention.

"I am perfectly prepared," he said, "to help the Grand Duke, and may I say before we go any further that I personally as an Englishman deeply deplore the manner in which the Tsar and Tsarina were treated by King George!"

"That does not bring them back to life or erase the hideous manner in which they were assassinated," Princess Militsa said.

"I agree," the Duke replied, "but there is nothing we can do for them now. However, I intend, if it is humanly possible, to save the Grand Duke and you, but we shall have to be intelligent about it."

The Prince moved nearer to him, but the Princess stayed where she was.

"I have to think this out carefully," the Duke said. "For the moment, I think the best thing would be for me to hire a car, which I believe is possible, and announce that I am going sight-seeing."

He spoke slowly, as if he was planning it out move by move as Harry had seen him plan a miiltary campaign in the desert.

"Is there a wood near here?" he asked unexpectedly.

"Yes," the Prince answered, "there is a small wood a little way from this house. A side-road leading off the main highway passes through the centre of it and the trees grow down to the edge."

"Good!" the Duke exclaimed. "Now what you have to do is to get His Royal Highness as far as the wood."

"He is very ill," the Princess said in a low voice. "He ought not to be moved."

"We have to move him!" Prince Ivan answered sharply.

She lapsed into silence and the Duke continued:

"I will collect you in the car, and will arrange for the other members of the yacht-party, which includes two women, to go shopping. If anybody is watching the yacht, they will see five people leave and five return, and we hope they will not realise there is a woman short."

The Prince waited for an explanation and the Duke said:

"I will bring with me in the car a yachting-cap for the Grand Duke like the one I shall be wearing myself, and an overcoat to cover him. He will take the place of my friend here, Sir Harold Nuneaton. The Princess will be provided with a hat, a scarf, and a coat, which, if she hurries aboard, will make her look like one of my women guests who will have been left in the town. There will also be clothes for you and Prince Alexander."

They were all listening intently and the Duke went on:

"Harry will wait with the others and later they will join the yacht by boat. You four will be safely aboard before Harry and the rest of my party climb up a rope-ladder on the opposite side of the ship. It will be difficult for anyone watching to see them, and if they do, it will be too late to do anything about it!"

He glanced at Harry before he added:

"If as a British subject one of my guests should be shot, I assure you it will cause an international scandal."

"It sounds an excellent idea, Your Grace," the Prince answered, "but it means we have to allow you to leave here, trusting you to come back."

"I can only give you my word," the Duke replied, "that I shall be with you tomorrow morning, shall we say at about eleven o'clock? I think to be very early or very late is bound to cause more attention than if we moved about at the busiest time of the day."

Prince Ivan nodded, and the Duke rose to his feet.

"Now," he said, "I would like to meet the Grand Duke. I have a feeling that however sceptical you three may be, he will trust me."

He walked towards the door against which the Princess was standing.

For a moment she did not move, and the Duke had the feeling that she wished to prevent him from seeing her father.

Then as his eyes met hers, she capitulated and moved aside.

The Duke opened the door and walked into a room that was nearly as large as the one he had just left, but just as empty, with the exception that lying on a bundle of rags, sacks, and straw was an elderly man.

It was difficult for him to recognise the Grand

Duke, whom he had last seen resplendent in the uniform of a Field Marshal and blazing with decorations at a Ball given at the Winter Palace.

Over six feet two inches in height, he had been a commanding figure who had won the admiration not only of the women he attracted but of the men he commanded.

Now he seemed to have shrunk, his hair was dead white, and his high cheek-bones were sharply prominent. But he was still good-looking, and, unlike the younger men, he had an aura of authority about him which was not weakened by either the rags he wore or by the rags on which he lay.

As the Duke approached him he put out his hand.

"I remember Your Grace," he said in a weak voice, "but we meet in very different circumstances."

"Very different, Your Royal Highness," the Duke agreed, "but I have devised a plan, which I have told Prince Ivan and your daughter, by which we can get you on board my yacht and carry you to safety."

The Grand Duke's hand was very cold, almost as if the shadow of death was upon him, but there was a warmth in his voice as he replied:

"I thank you. I do not worry for myself but for my daughter. She is young and our sufferings these last three years have been almost intolerable."

"I can understand your feelings," the Duke replied, "but I believe, Your Royal Highness, that the worst is now behind you, and you must trust me to get you away from here as quickly as possible."

The Duke knew that the others were listening for the answer the Grand Duke would give.

"I trust you, Buckminster," he said, "not with my life, which is unimportant, but with the lives of these three young people."

The Duke bowed his head in the correct fashion accorded to Royalty.

Then as he saw the Grand Duke's eyes close as if he was very tired, he turned and walked back into the other room.

"As His Royal Highness trusts me," he said as the Princess closed the door, "I presume you will do the same?"

"I hope you will not betray us," the Prince said. "But you must realise that one unwary word, one whisper of where we are, and tomorrow if you come to collect us we shall all be dead!"

The Duke did not reply to this. He merely walked to the wooden box on which Harry had been sitting.

On the Duke's instructions, when they had left the yacht he had been carrying a parcel which he had tucked under his arm. It was wrapped up in brown paper and the Duke now picked it up off the floor.

"I remembered when I was coming to see Your Highness," he said to Prince Ivan, "that it is a Russian custom that a guest should always arrive with a present for his host. I have brought you something I thought you might appreciate, and I hope you will accept it."

The Prince frowned for a moment as if he thought the Duke was deliberately underlining his own inhospitable reception.

Then with a sudden change of mood he smiled, and despite his beard it made him look as young as he was in actual years.

"I thank Your Grace, and although I have no idea what your present can be, I can assure you I accept it with gratitude."

"Now I think we should return," the Duke said. "There are a great many plans to make before eleven o'clock tomorrow morning."

The Prince gave a little laugh that somehow seemed strange after the solemnity of the way they had been talking up until now.

"The carriage awaits Your Grace," he announced, "and here is your coachman!"

As he spoke he made a gesture with his hand towards Prince Alexander, who grinned.

"We would not dare trust anyone else," the Prince explained, "and naturally we borrowed the carriage and horse without its owner's knowledge. I can only pray they will not hang us for horse-stealing!"

"That would be an unnecessary disaster!" the Duke agreed lightly.

Prince Alexander hurried away and the Duke turned to the Princess, who was standing near the door to her father's room.

"Good-night, Your Serene Highness," he said with a Royal bow.

"Good-night, Your Grace," she replied.

Her voice was as cold and distant as it had been before, and he had the feeling, although it seemed quite unreasonable, that she was hating him.

Then the Prince escorted them down the dark passage to the front door and peeped through it, until the carriage appeared.

"This house was empty," he said in a low voice, "and we hope that no-one knows it is now occupied."

That was what the Duke had suspected, but at that moment the carriage came down the road from where Prince Alexander had hidden it.

"Good-night," he said, then hurried down the path, followed by Harry, and opened the door and stepped inside the carriage almost before the horse came to a standstill.

As they drove away Harry made a sound which was one of relief and astonishment combined.

"I certainly did not expect anything like that when we set out this evening," he said.

"Poor devils!" the Duke remarked. "I could barely recognise Kerenski."

"I am not surprised! Do not forget when you send them clothes tomorrow they will also need a razor."

"I think they have one," the Duke answered. "The Grand Duke's beard is very much the same as it was in the old days, only now his hair is white."

"I suppose with those ragged clothes a beard is a disguise."

"An effective one. I believe their own mothers

would not recognise them if they saw them in the street."

"As you say—poor devils! What they must have gone through!" Harry said. "And all four of them look as if they are starving"

"Well, they will have something to eat tonight at any rate," the Duke said.

"What did you put in the parcel?" Harry asked.

"Only things which I thought were not likely to insult them," the Duke answered, "but in the circumstances bread and perhaps some cooked meats would have been more sensible."

"What *did* you give them?" Harry enquired.

"Pâté de foie gras and caviar!" the Duke answered.

"My God, when they eat that, it will inevitably make them feel a sentimental nostalgia for the 'good old days.'"

"I think it is more important that it will keep them from dying of starvation until tomorrow at any rate!" the Duke answered.

They drove in silence for a little while, until as they neared the yacht Harry said:

"I felt damned uncomfortable when they spoke like that about the King refusing to let the Tsar and Tsarina come to England, and I do not suppose any Russian aristocrats left alive will ever forgive us."

"It is most unlikely," the Duke agreed.

As he spoke, he was thinking of the anger and bitterness in Princess Militsa's voice.

Chapter Three

The Duke and Harry sat up late, talking over their plans, and when Harry finally got to bed he thought it was many years since he had known Buck to be so animated or so enthusiastic about anything.

"What he always needs is some difficult project to keep him interested," he told himself.

He thought, as he had often done before, that if anyone with brains was overwhelmingly rich it was not always an asset.

They had decided that they would not say anything to the rest of the party until the last moment.

"If they kept talking it over amongst themselves," the Duke said wisely, "the stewards will overhear, and I have always believed that servants carry gossip quicker than the pigeons did at the time of the Napoleonic Wars."

They all breakfasted together as usual, and Dolly enquired half-heartedly what plans the Duke had for them today.

"If the sight-seeing is going to be like it was yesterday, with the exception of the jewels in the Sultan's Palace," she said, "I would rather do something else."

"I have a plan," the Duke said, "but I will tell you about it after breakfast."

Dolly looked at him enquiringly but Harry attracted her attention by describing the jewels she would undoubtedly be able to buy in Cairo.

When breakfast was finished the Duke said:

"I want to talk to you in my cabin. Will you all come along there?"

"What's up?" Lord Radstock enquired.

As the Duke did not answer him, they all trooped to where the Duke's special cabin was situated amidships.

He sat down at his desk and only when the door was shut did he say:

"I have something very important to tell you."

Before he could go any further, Dolly interrupted:

"You look just like a School-master giving a lecture at the end of term. I feel quite certain my report is going to be a bad one."

"That of course depends on you," the Duke replied.

Because he spoke in a serious tone, both Dolly and Nancy looked at him questioningly.

"I have asked you to come in here where we shall not be overheard," he went on, "because I am going to ask you today to act a part which, if it is badly done, could have very serious consequences."

His guests, who did not know what he was talking about, looked puzzled and he went on:

"We have a chance to save the lives of several people, but one false step, one careless word, could result, and I am not being melodramatic, in their deaths."

"Are you serious?" Dolly asked.

"Very serious!"

"I cannot believe it!" she cried. "Are you telling me you are in the Secret Service or something like that?"

"Perhaps in a way it is something like that," the Duke said, "and I am asking for your co-operation."

"Of course, dear Buck, you have that whole-heartedly!" Nancy cried. "Just tell us what you want us to do and we will do it."

"Very well," the Duke said.

He lowered his voice as if even in his private cabin he was afraid of eaves-droppers.

"I have sent one of my staff," he said "to procure an open car which I shall drive myself. That is the first step."

"Where are we going?" Dolly asked.

"We will leave here at quarter-to-eleven as if we were going on a sight-seeing trip."

He paused, as if he expected an interruption, but as they were all listening intently he went on:

"When we get to the Galata Bridge, Harry will take you beneath it where there are a number of stalls at which you will appear interested and will buy anything that takes your fancy."

"From what I saw yesterday in the Bazaar, I should think that is very little," Dolly remarked.

"I agree it will be rubbish," the Duke said, "nevertheless, you will make a number of purchases which Harry will pay for. Then George will suggest that you hire a boat, and it will seem a good idea!"

"Why?" Dolly asked.

The Duke ignored the question and went on:

"When a boat has been found, you will all get into it. On Harry's instructions it will take you round the harbour to where we are moored. You will approach the yacht and board it by climbing up the rope-ladders that will be let down on the seaward side."

Nancy gave a little cry of excitement.

"I have never heard anything so intriguing!" she exclaimed. "And what will you be doing in the meantime?"

"That you will learn later," the Duke answered. "I expect to be on board soon after you get back."

"Then what do we do?"

"The yacht will leave immediately," the Duke answered. "We are going to Cairo."

"But I do not understand," Dolly said. "What about the people whose lives we are saving?"

"You will meet them in due course," the Duke replied, "but I wish to impress upon you that this is not a joke or a game. It is a deadly serious operation, and if any of you act at all unnaturally or suspiciously or say anything indiscreet, it might prove disastrous!"

"Are you saying," Dolly asked, "that people, or 'spies' is the right word I suppose, may be listening to us—watching us?"

"That is a distinct possibility."

"It sounds creepy and rather frightening."

"Nothing need frighten you," the Duke said reassuringly, "if you do exactly what I have told you to do."

"We will try, we will certainly try not to let you down," Nancy promised, "and personally I find the whole thing thrilling!"

"Let us go and get ready," Dolly said, as if she wanted something else to do.

"Be careful to say nothing in front of the stewards," the Duke warned. "In fact, I forbid any of you to speak of this again until we are steaming away from the city towards the open sea."

Dolly walked up to the Duke, kissed his cheek, and said:

"You certainly think of original ways to keep us amused, darling. I rather like you in the role of 'Bulldog Drummond'!"

The Duke smiled, but as she and Nancy left the cabin he said to George Radstock:

"Wait a minute, George!"

The women were out of ear-shot and the Duke said:

"Do you think you could get hold of one of your wife's hats, a long coat, and also a scarf—the type she would wear if she was going in an open car?"

"Yes, of course," Lord Radstock answered.

The Duke hesitated, then he said:

"I would rather she did not know I need them; but if that is impossible, then ask her not to tell Dolly."

There was a faint smile of understanding on George Radstock's lips as he said:

"I understand. Where shall I bring the things?"

"Put them in Harry's cabin," the Duke replied.

George hurried after his wife, and Harry said:

"I think that was sensible of you, Buck. Dolly is not going to like having another woman on board."

"That is what I thought," the Duke replied drily.

He was in fact thinking that in an adventure of this sort, the last person he would have wanted to participate was Dolly.

She was impetuous, impulsive, unreliable, and insanely jealous.

There would be no good cause for her to be jealous over Princess Militsa, who had shown already that she disliked him. But the mere fact that she was a woman would be enough to upset Dolly, and the less she knew about the Russians until they were safely aboard, the better.

From the Duke's point of view it was difficult to possess his soul in patience until it was time to leave.

Last night he had consulted with Harry over the clothes they would need to disguise the Grand Duke and the rest of his party.

"My trousers will be the right length because both the Princes are very tall," the Duke had said, "but as I imagine they are abnormally thin under those rags, your yachting-jacket will fit them better than mine."

"I only have one spare one," Harry replied.

"Well, luckily I have several," the Duke said. "I have had to trust my valet with what I need, but as I have trusted him with my own life on many occasions I know he is as safe as houses."

Harry knew that the Duke's valet, Dawkins, had been with him in the war, and as he revered his Master he would do anything that was asked of him.

"What Dawkins has suggested," the Duke went on, "is that he should put the clothes in a large picnic-basket. If there is anyone watching us he will think we are driving outside the city, and when we return quite soon he will merely assume we have changed our minds."

"That is a good idea!" Harry approved.

"The only difficulty now is shoes," the Duke went on, "although I think the Russians will take the same size as I do myself, or perhaps something a little smaller."

"You can have two pairs of mine," Harry said. "I think I take a size smaller than you."

"I'll tell Dawkins," the Duke said. "You will find that everything we require is being accumulated in your cabin."

There was no need for him to add that that was the one place where Dolly was not likely to see it.

An hour later, talking and laughing gaily, they went down the gang-plank to where waiting for them on the Quay was an ancient but large open touring-car.

It was a German make which had once been an expensive vehicle, and it had been left behind after the war.

The Duke amongst his other achievements was an experienced driver and had often competed in the speed-races at Brooklands.

He got behind the wheel, saying jokingly:

"I hope, being somewhat 'long in the tooth,' it will not strand us in some outlandish place!"

Dolly by right got in beside him, while the three others sat on the back seat.

The picnic-basket was strapped behind on the luggage-grid and they were off.

"Do you think anyone was watching us?" Dolly asked as they left the Quay.

"One never knows," the Duke replied, "and remember that when you are under the bridge, anyone in the crowd could be watching you for very much more sinister reasons than that you are very beautiful."

Dolly preened herself.

"I want you to think me beautiful, Buck," she said, "but sometimes you are tardy in telling me so."

"I will make up for it when we have left Constantinople!" he said. "I dislike the place and I am sure we shall enjoy Cairo much more. You will perhaps be able to find there the emeralds you have set your heart on!"

"Oh, Buck, do you mean that? How divine of you! I am longing to have some emeralds, and the bigger the better!"

Cynically the Duke told himself that he was deliberately bribing Dolly into a good humour, and he despised himself for doing so.

But there was too much at stake to risk her being in one of her difficult moods, and as he felt her hand on his knee, he knew that the thought of the emeralds would undoubtedly smooth over the rough moments ahead when she met Princess Militsa.

They arrived at the Galata Bridge and the Duke drove the car to the end of it where there were steps for people who wished to go down to sea-level.

The Duke gave Harry some instructions, then as they moved away casually he drove on, as if he was intent on finding somewhere to park the car.

It was not easy to move quickly through the narrow streets of the Galata district but he achieved it, and soon he was on the road where they had been last night.

As he passed the house in which they had met the Grand Duke, he thought it looked empty and desolate, which was encouraging.

He drove farther up the road and found the lane that the Prince had described to him and the trees growing down to the very edge of it.

He stopped the car, thought for a moment that there was no-one in sight and wondered if he had dreamt the whole episode or, worse still, the Russians had been discovered and killed, as they were afraid they might be.

Then when the trees were thickest Prince Alexander appeared.

At first sight of him the Duke jumped out of the car and started to undo the rope which held the picnic-basket on the luggage-grid.

Prince Alexander helped him, and only as they lifted it from the grid did the Duke speak for the first time.

"How is His Royal Highness?"

"Very weak."

The Duke put his hand in his pocket and drew out a flask.

"I thought he would need this."

"Thank you," Prince Alexander replied.

He picked up the picnic-basket and started to walk back the way he had come.

The Duke wondered if he should offer to assist him but felt he might feel insulted. In fact, before he reached the shelter of the trees, Prince Ivan appeared to help with the basket.

They disappeared and the Duke started up the car and edged it nearer to the trees.

There was no-one about; and the sun seeping through the branches was warm but still not strong enough to melt the snow which lay on the sides of the roads and in the wood.

The Duke looked back and from where he was standing he had a magnificent view of the Golden Horn, and how the city straddled Europe and Asia while the high minarets of the Suleiman Mosque protectively overlooked the meeting of the waters.

The sea was blue and the city had the beauty and glory which had captivated and inspired artists since the time of the Crusades.

The Duke thought, not for the first time, that it was a pity the Turks had been on the wrong side in the last war. It would take longer than it need have done to bring them back to prosperity.

He had been waiting what seemed a long time, and he looked anxiously up and down the lane in case there was anyone about. But it appeared deserted and the only traffic was on the road he had left.

At last, when he was wondering if he should go to see what had happened, he saw figures coming from between the trees.

The two Princes were supporting the Grand Duke, and as they all were now wearing yachting-clothes, the Duke thought that at a quick glance they could quite easily be the party he had left at the Galata Bridge.

Wearing Nancy's coat and hat, with a long blue

chiffon scarf swathed over it and falling over her shoulders, Princess Militsa looked very different from the scarecrow she had seemed last night.

But, in the need to move quickly, he barely noticed it.

The Duke helped the Princes get the Grand Duke into the back seat, and one look at His Royal Highness's bloodless face was enough to tell that he was already exhausted by the effort.

"Give him some more brandy!" the Duke said sharply.

He realised that while he had been helping with the Grand Duke, the Princess had got into the front seat of the car.

Without speaking, he started up the engine, put it in gear, and with a sense of relief moved off.

Although everything had gone smoothly up until now, he had been anxious in case the hired car would not start.

He drove to the end of the road before turning round, then drove back the way he had come, crossing over the Galata Bridge without even wondering what had happened to Dolly and the rest, intent only on getting back to the yacht as quickly as possible.

As usual there was a confusion of horse-drawn drays and pedestrians who seemed intent on committing suicide. It was only as he drove down a comparatively empty road to the Quay that the Duke had a moment to glance at the silent passenger at his side.

She was staring straight ahead and he realised that her profile was almost Grecian. The firm line of her nose might have been the model for Aphrodite, although the sharpness of her chin betrayed how undernourished she was.

When they reached the Quay and bumped over the cobblestones, the Duke brought the car as near to the yacht as he could.

Without being told to, the Princes hurried to get the Grand Duke out of the back seat and take him with some difficulty up the narrow gang plank onto the deck.

Dawkins, as already instructed by the Duke, was

waiting for them, and only as all four disappeared inside did the Duke give a sigh of relief and move the car, which he had kept running, to the other side of the Quay.

Then, deliberately sauntering in a casual manner, he walked up the gangplank and went inside also, where Stevens was waiting to take his cap.

"Is the rest of the party aboard, Stevens?" the Duke enquired.

"Yes, Your Grace."

"Then tell the Captain we are ready to leave immediately."

"I think he's aware of that, Your Grace."

As the steward spoke, the yacht began to move away from the Quay and the Duke could hear the vibration of the engines.

The next moment Harry came from the Saloon.

"We've done it!" he exclaimed.

The Duke nodded.

"Everything went according to plan, but the sooner we get into the Sea of Marmara, the better."

"I agree with you," Harry said, "but I cannot imagine that anyone would dare to stop us."

"One never knows," the Duke replied.

He walked into the Saloon, where the rest of the party were obviously waiting for him to give them an explanation.

Dolly jumped to her feet.

"I simply must ask you what all this is about," she said. "As you can imagine, I am consumed with curiosity, and it was really very rough in the boat. I thought I might be sea-sick."

It was just like Dolly to find something to complain about, the Duke thought, but he was so delighted at the success of his plan that he found it difficult to be critical.

"You must tell us who those men are who have just come aboard," Nancy said, "and the woman."

She spoke without thinking, and Dolly looked at her sharply and asked:

"Woman?—what woman? Nobody said anything to me about a woman!"

"I was looking out the port-hole," Nancy replied, "and I thought I saw three men in yachting-clothes followed by—a woman."

She looked apologetically at the Duke as she spoke, and he knew she had not meant to be indiscreet but had thought that as everyone was aboard there was no longer any reason for secrecy.

"You didn't tell me," Dolly said almost indignantly, "that you had invited so many people to join us—and who is this woman anyway?"

Without answering, the Duke walked across to the port-hole.

The ship was gathering speed and now they were well away from the shore and moving towards the open sea.

He knew it would not be long before he need have no more apprehension and the Grand Duke would be, to all intents and purposes, as safe as he would be in Cairo.

"I am waiting, Buck," Dolly persisted, and now there was an undoubted edge to her voice.

The Duke turned from the port-hole.

"Forgive me while I just find out if our guests have everything they require," he replied, "then I will tell you everything you wish to know."

He heard Dolly give a cry of protest as he left the Saloon to go below to the cabins.

He had instructed Stevens to place the Grand Duke in the largest and best cabin that was not being used, and he found him now lying on the bed, with one of the Princes taking off his shoes and the Princess holding a glass of brandy to his lips.

Stevens was standing near the door, and as he entered the cabin the Duke asked sharply:

"You have the soup ready and the other food I ordered?"

"It's coming now, Your Grace," Stevens replied.

As he spoke, he glanced past the Duke to where two stewards carrying trays were waiting to enter the cabin.

They set the trays down on a side-table and the Duke said:

"I think what will help His Royal Highness better than anything else is the soup I have ordered, and I imagine you will all appreciate some substantial 'elevenses' after the anxiety of the last few hours."

He smiled at them as he spoke, then followed the stewards from the cabin.

He understood that the Russians, in their state of near-starvation, would not wish to eat for the first time in front of other people.

He had therefore instructed the stewards to tell the Chef that what would be required the moment they arrived was a really nourishing soup made from beef, chicken, and game if it was procurable, besides pâtés, vol-au-vents, and other snacks that were quick to consume and easy to digest.

He did not provide any wine or spirits, which he thought would be disastrous on an empty stomach, but instead had ordered tea, which he thought the Russians would prefer, as it was almost a national drink, with coffee in case they had developed European tastes.

Satisfied that he had shown forethought, the Duke went back again to the Saloon.

As he entered he saw that Dolly was pouting and he told himself he was bored with her.

He decided to ignore her pretty but petulant face and spoke instead to Nancy.

"I can now tell you what you want to know."

"You can imagine we are bursting with curiosity," Nancy replied.

"I know that," the Duke answered, "but it really was important that you should know nothing until my new guests were safe, which I now believe them to be."

The Duke had the feeling that because it had been so nerve-racking, he should touch wood.

He told himself that the Grand Duke was as it were on British soil and it was doubtful, however much pressure the Soviet spies might try to exert on the Turks, that they would be prepared to interfere.

He walked to the end of the Saloon, appreciating that Nancy and George were giving him their rapt attention and so was Dolly although she pretended otherwise.

Only Harry had a faint twinkle in his eyes, as if he knew that the Duke was still enjoying the drama of what had occurred.

"My chief guest, whom I have just got on board, with considerable difficulty and your very valuable help," he began, "is the Grand Duke Alexis of Russia."

There was an audible gasp and George Radstock said:

"I thought he had been assassinated!"

"So did I," the Duke replied, "but he is in fact alive and has been in hiding all these years since the Revolution. However, he is in a very weak condition from starvation."

"How terrible for him!" Nancy said. "But how can he have survived?"

"In the South of Russia they are not so loyal to the Revolution as in the North," the Duke answered, "and his own people were able to help him, even against the Bolsheviks who were determined that he should die."

"And now he is safe?" Nancy enquired.

"He is safe!" the Duke repeated as if he confirmed it to himself. "And so is his nephew, Prince Alexander Saronov, and Prince Ivan Kerenski, whom I knew when I was in Russia."

"And the woman?"

Dolly's voice rang out sharply.

"She is the Grand Duke's daughter," the Duke answered, "Her Serene Highness Princess Militsa."

He thought for a moment that Dolly was impressed that their last guest was so distinguished. Then she said:

"She must be a tough creature to have endured such hardship."

There was no doubt that she implied that the Princess was unfeminine, but Nancy said:

"Poor woman! Is there anything I can do to help her?"

"I feel certain she will be grateful for your help

later," the Duke answered, "but for the moment I have left them alone, first to the realisation that they are no longer in danger, and second to the very different conditions they will find here from those Harry and I found them in last night."

"You saw them last night?" Dolly asked. "Why did you not tell me?"

"Because, as I have said, it was a secret, and the fewer people who knew that they even existed, the better, from their point of view."

"I was not likely to betray them," Dolly said.

"Not deliberately, of course," the Duke agreed, "but you might have done so inadvertently."

"Really, Buck! You talk to me as if I were half-witted!" Dolly remarked disagreeably.

The Duke knew that she was annoyed because other people had joined the party and that she was determined to pick a quarrel with him. Harry wondered how she could be such a fool.

The Duke, however, was too pleased with himself at the moment to take much notice of Dolly and her behaviour. Instead he said:

"After a somewhat serious morning, but nevertheless a very successful one, I think we all deserve a drink! Ring the bell, Harry. I don't know about you, but I could do with a glass of champagne!"

"Well, I certainly need one," Dolly exclaimed, "after pitching and tossing in a boat that smelt of fish, and being kept in the dark about secrets which I consider I had every right to be told!"

"The Duke and I were creeping about in disguise, Dolly," Harry said, "and you are far too beautiful not to be noticed, even if we dressed you up in a *yashmak*."

He was trying to coax her back into a good humour, and because she enjoyed compliments, she gave him a smile before she said:

"I thought once of giving a party with every woman veiled except for me. Then I thought Buck would find it an irresistible temptation to lift their veils."

"He has always been curious," Harry said, "but in

this case with excellent results. I don't mind telling
you all that it was Buck's brilliant plan which has
saved the Grand Duke and the others from the death
which the Bolsheviks had planned for them."

"That sounds just like you, Buck," George Radstock said. "I only wish you had let me in on the
secret. It sounds to me exactly like a story by Phillips
Oppenheim."

"That is what it has been!" Harry laughed. "And
when we get to Cairo there will be a happy ending."

"Why?" Dolly enquired.

"Because Prince Ivan has friends there who he
thinks will find him some sort of employment, and
Prince Alexander intends to join the Foreign Legion."

"The Foreign Legion!" Nancy exclaimed. "How
romantic!"

It was nearly one o'clock and they were moving
smoothly through the Sea of Marmara when the Duke
sent Harry down below to say that he hoped his
guests, with the possible exception of the Grand
Duke, would join them for luncheon.

The Duke had been aware when he saw them
as they came from the wood that they had both
shaved off their beards, but he had not realised what
a difference it would make, or that in his smart yachting-clothes they bore no resemblance to the ragged,
rough peasants he had seen last night in the empty
house.

Now, except that he looked desperately thin and
ill, Prince Ivan seemed to have regained his charm
and a little of the dash that had made him such an
outstanding figure in St. Petersburg.

There was no doubt that Prince Alexander too
was an extremely handsome young man.

As Harry came back accompanied by the Princes,
the Duke walked towards them.

"Let me welcome you aboard, Your Highness,"
he said to Prince Ivan, "and we all hope that this
will be the beginning of a new chapter and a very
much happier one in all your lives."

"It is difficult for me to express my gratitude,
Your Grace . . ." the Prince began.

"Then please do not try," the Duke interrupted.
"Let me present my party."

He introduced Dolly first, then Lord and Lady
Radstock.

Then when he had presented them to Prince
Alexander and they had all begun to talk, he said in
a low voice to Harry:

"What about the Princess?"

"She wishes to stay with her father. Dawkins has
got the Grand Duke into bed. He has had something
to eat and is now resting."

"I should have thought Dawkins could have
looked after him while the Princess joined us for
luncheon."

"Yes, he suggested that," Harry replied, "but she
refused. She may be shy, I do not know."

"Ask Nancy to go down and see her," the Duke
suggested.

Harry understood that it was something the Duke
did not wish to do himself, so he spoke to Nancy and
she hurried from the Saloon.

She returned only a few minutes before it was
announced that luncheon was served, and she was
alone.

"She is charming," she said to the Duke in a low
voice, "but we will talk about it later."

She glanced towards Dolly as she spoke, and the
Duke understood that it would be wise not to raise
the matter of the Princess for the moment.

It was in fact several hours later before the
Duke went out alone on deck and was followed by
Nancy Radstock.

The sun was still shining but now the wind was
blustery and cold and Nancy was wearing a thick
coat with a fur-trimmed hood.

"I am glad we have left Constantinople behind,"
she said. "The poverty there made me miserable, and
the empty Palaces gave me the creeps even before I
learnt about the suffering of your Russians."

"You spoke to the Princess?" the Duke asked.

"She said she did not wish to leave her father

and join us for luncheon," Nancy replied. "I think too there were other reasons.

"What were they?"

"The first is that having been starved for so long and then being plied with food when she arrived on the yacht, it was impossible for her to eat any more."

Nancy smiled and put her hand on the Duke's arm.

"That was considerate of you, Buck. I never expected you to be so understanding where suffering was concerned."

"Go on with what you were telling me," the Duke said, as if he felt embarrassed at her praise.

"I think the Princess is acutely conscious of having nothing to wear."

He turned to look at Nancy.

"But surely . . ." he began.

"Yes, of course. I offered her anything she wanted. She accepted a nightgown and said that otherwise she would wear what she owned."

The Duke stared at her incredulously.

"But surely . . ." he began.

He remembered the ghastly ragged garments the Princess had been wearing when she had called at the yacht and last night in the empty house.

"She has a dress that she is wearing now," Nancy said, "which must have been an expensive model in perhaps 1916, though it is now threadbare, darned, and looks a little strange. But it is hers."

"I suppose it is what I should have expected," the Duke said in a low voice. "You will have to get round it somehow, Nancy."

"I do not know how I can," Nancy replied. "She is very firm on the subject. 'You are most kind, Lady Radstock,' she said, 'but you must understand that in all these years I have not begged, borrowed, or stolen, and I do not intend to start now!'"

The Duke looked slightly sceptical and Nancy said:

"I gather, from what she told me, that she worked in some way or other, as did the Princes, for

the food they obtained from the peasants before they
managed to leave Russia."

"What kind of work?"

"I gather, although she was not explicit, that the
Princess cooked and even scrubbed floors for anyone
who would employ her, and the Princes worked on
the land. If you look at Prince Ivan's hands you will
see there is no doubt of the way he has toiled so that
they could eat."

The Duke leant over the rail and looked out to
sea.

He was thinking that the Russians had ideals
and principles which most English people and certainly those of any other nation would think absurd.
Yet, one could not help admiring them for refusing
to lower themselves to the level of more ordinary
human beings.

"What can we do, Nancy?" he asked, and she
knew he was worrying over the Princess.

"I will try to think of something," she promised,
"but it is not going to be easy, and, Buck . . ."

It was the way Nancy said his name which made
the Duke look round enquiringly.

There was a pause. Then Nancy said:

"I suppose you realise that when she does not
look so ill or so emaciated, the Princess is very beautiful?"

The Duke did not answer.

He was only thinking that despite his promise of
emeralds, Dolly, when she saw the Princess, was
bound to be difficult.

Chapter Four

The Duke, as he usually did, spent a great deal of the day on the bridge beside the Captain.

He enjoyed navigating his own yacht and he also found it a relief to get away from the chatter of his women-guests, which actually meant Dolly.

She had been petulant during luncheon and would have been more so had not Prince Ivan put himself out to exert the charm that had been so characteristic of him in the old days.

There was no doubt that the two Princes were finding it a joy beyond words to be in civilised surroundings, apart from the fact that they appreciated the excellent food and drink which had been denied them for so long.

The Duke liked the fact that they did not speak of their sufferings, but the terrible experiences they had been through were only too obvious in the thinness of their bodies, the sallowness of their skin, and the condition of their hands, which revealed the manual labour they had been forced to do.

They were wearing the Duke's clothes, which even if too large for them made them appear the gentlemen they were, and they seemed to merge easily with the other guests and might in fact have known no other life but one of carefree luxury.

However, the Duke was acutely aware that there was one member of the party missing, and that was the Princess.

She was well enough in health to join them, and

63

it irritated him to think that he could not overcome
her prejudice and persuade her to be as sociable as
the Princes were.

He guessed that after she had eaten with her
father, the Grand Duke would undoubtedly rest during the first part of the afternoon and she would do
the same.

He therefore waited until after tea had been
served in the Saloon, and Dolly was intent on playing Mah-jong, before he slipped away as if he were
going to his own cabin.

As he reached the door of the Saloon, Dolly
called out:

"Don't leave us, Buck. I want to dance when I
have finished this game."

"I shall not be long," the Duke replied vaguely,
"and you have plenty of partners without me."

There was no denying this, although the Duke
suspected that the Princes would rather relax as
they were doing at the moment on comfortable sofas,
reading English, French, and Turkish newspapers
which they found absorbingly interesting.

When they were not amusing Dolly and Nancy
they plied the Duke and Harry with questions about
the state of Europe, social and political conditions
after the war—in fact everything that had happened
of which they had no knowledge whatsoever.

"Quite frankly," the Duke heard Harry say, "the
politicians have made a mess of the peace," and he
thought unhappily that this was true.

But for the moment he was concerned with
Princess Militsa, and as he went down below to the
Grand Duke's cabin he was wondering what would
be the best way to approach her and make her realise
that her pride was unnecessary.

When he reached the cabin, Dawkins was just
coming out with a tray in his hands.

He stood aside to make way and the Duke
walked in, saying:

"I hope Your Royal Highness will allow me to
visit you?"

The Grand Duke, who was sitting up in bed, propped up against his pillows, smiled in response.

The Princess, who had been sitting by his bedside, rose to her feet and the Duke thought there was not only no welcome in her eyes but definitely an expression he recognised.

It gave him a strange feeling to know that there was a woman, any woman, who actually hated him.

He was so used to seeing a gleam of admiration when a woman looked at him, and one which told him only too clearly that she wished to attract him.

Now it was almost like being plunged into cold water to find that here was someone very different.

He walked towards the bed.

"I hope Your Royal Highness is feeling better."

"I cannot tell you what a delight it is," the Grand Duke replied, "to sleep between linen sheets and on a comfortable mattress."

The Duke sat down on the chair the Princess had vacated.

"I found in the war," he said, "though my experiences were certainly not as traumatic as yours, that what I missed were little things which I had always taken for granted until I was suddenly deprived of them."

The Grand Duke smiled and the Duke turned to look at the Princess.

"I hope Your Serene Highness has everything you require?"

"Everything," she replied in a low voice.

The Duke realised that she was wearing the worn dress that Nancy had described to him.

He could see that it was threadbare in many places, darned until the material itself had frayed away to nothing, and the colour, which had once been a deep blue, was nothing more than drab grey.

It was a very simple gown made with a "V" neck which must once have had a white collar. The dress hung straight to the ground with the exception of a wide belt.

It struck him that it was a very young girl's dress

and he remembered that the Princess had been only thirteen when the Revolution started.

He would not have known this if one of the Princes had not mentioned that she was a year older than the Tsarevich, and the Duke had realised that she was now twenty-two.

For six miserable years, when she should have been enjoying herself as young girls did while still in the School-Room and then emerging as débutantes, she had instead been fighting to stay alive.

Now she stood on the other side of her father's bed, and looking at her the Duke realised that Harry had been right when he had said she was beautiful.

There was nothing pretty about her, nothing of the Chocolate Box pink-and-white and gold-and-blue that made Dolly the personification of an "English Rose."

Instead she had an ageless classical beauty which the Greeks had tried to portray in their statues of goddesses.

Her face was thin, her cheek-bones seemed almost as if they might burst through her skin, and yet with her oval forehead and her huge eyes she had a strange, mystical beauty which he had never seen before.

He noticed that over her drab dress she wore a shawl which surprised him because it was dark red in colour and looked new.

He remembered that Nancy had said she wished only to wear her own clothes and thought it strange.

Then when he looked at the shawl again, trying to conceal that he was doing so, he realised that it was one of the cloths which had covered the small tables in the Saloon.

He thought Dawkins must have provided it for her, and he realised that because there was nothing personal about it the Princess had accepted it while she would not accept clothes that had been worn by an Englishwoman.

"Tell me what is happening in England," the Grand Duke asked.

The Duke knew that here was yet another guest

who was eager to have news of what had occurred in the world from which he had been isolated.

He told His Royal Highness many things he wanted to know.

Then when he was still talking he saw the Grand Duke's eyes close and realised that, old and tired, he had fallen asleep.

The Princess had moved to a far corner of the room, where she was sitting, the Duke thought deliberately, on an upright chair, and while he had been speaking to her father he had felt the vibrations coming from her as they had when she had sat beside him in the car.

He did not turn his head to look at her but nevertheless was conscious of her in a manner which he could not explain.

Now he rose to his feet and she came quickly to the bedside, putting her fingers to her lips in case he should speak to her.

She pulled the satin cover over her father's hands and the Duke knew that, however warm the cabin was, the Grand Duke in his emaciated state would still feel the cold.

He walked towards the door and when he reached it he deliberately stood waiting until the Princess turned her head to see why he had not left.

Then he beckoned to her.

He knew as she stared at him that she did not wish to obey his summons.

He opened the door and beckoned her again, and as if it was impossible for her to refuse, she came from the cabin into the passage outside.

"I want to speak to you," the Duke said.

"I cannot leave my . . . father."

The Duke had expected this reply, and he had already noticed that Dawkins was in an empty cabin next door with the door open.

He did not answer the Princess. He merely said to the valet in a low voice:

"Will you stay with His Royal Highness, Dawkins, until Her Serene Highness returns?"

"Yes, Your Grace."

It was impossible for the Princess to make any
further objections, and the Duke led the way to his
own special cabin, knowing as he did so that she
was following him reluctantly.

He entered it and he wondered if she was thinking of the first time they had met each other, when
she had brought Prince Ivan's letter and insisted on
seeing him personally despite everything that Stevens
had tried to do to prevent her intrusion.

The Duke indicated one of the comfortable
chairs.

"Will you sit down?" he invited.

The Princess obeyed, sitting not comfortably but
very upright and straight-backed on the edge of the
chair, her hands in her lap.

Her dark hair was swept back from her forehead into a large roll at the nape of her neck.

It was not in the least fashionable and was a
complete contrast to the fluffed-out curls which decorated Dolly's head, a style which was also followed
by Nancy.

And yet, the Duke thought, there was a rightness
about her appearance, which, strangely enough, was
not spoilt by her dress or the worn slippers he saw
peeping beneath the far-too-long skirt.

It suddenly struck him as a connoisseur of
women's fashions that the reason she sat so primly
was to hide her ankles because she wore no stockings.

He remembered noticing, the night he first saw
her, that under her ragged skirt her legs were bound
with strips of material almost as if they were ban-
daged.

It was how the Russian peasants kept out the
cold, and he was sure now that she could not afford
to buy stockings and therefore used her long dress
to conceal her naked legs.

It seemed inconceivable that any woman could
be so proud when after the years of destitution she
had been offered gowns in the very latest fashion.

But there was a stormy expression in the Princess's eyes which told him that, like her countrymen

in battle, she would rather die than surrender or in
this case lower her principles.

"I want to talk to you about your father," the
Duke said aloud.

The expression on the Princess's face softened
immediately.

"I feel sure," he went on, "that with good food
and careful nursing he will soon look as he did when
I last saw him in St. Petersburg, one of the most handsome and outstanding men in the whole Court."

"He is very . . . weak," the Princess said in a low
voice.

"That is understandable," the Duke agreed, "but
when we get to Alexandria he must see the best doctor available, and you will be able to find out if
there is anything wrong that cannot be healed by
time and care."

The Princess did not speak but the Duke could
read her thoughts and knew she was wondering how
they could afford the services of the best Doctor.

He wanted to tell her to stop worrying and leave
everything to him, but instead he said:

"I also want to talk to you about yourself."

He saw the Princess stiffen and the hostility was
back in her face.

"I understand," the Duke said, picking his words
carefully, "that you refused Lady Radstock's offer to
lend you anything you required. I am only hoping
that does not extend to refusing the use of an overcoat
should you go out on deck."

Now he waited for a reply, and after a moment,
almost as if it was dragged from her lips, the Princess
said:

"I have to . . . look after my . . . father."

"Of course," the Duke agreed. "At the same time,
you cannot be so foolish as not to realise that you
need fresh air and a certain amount of exercise."

He felt that she was going to tell him politely to
mind his own business, but he went on:

"While I am perfectly prepared to nurse one in-
valid, you must be aware that it would be extremely
inconvenient to have two on my hands."

"I will not ... inconvenience you, Your Grace," the Princess said.

"How can you be sure of that?" the Duke asked. "When one is weak from want of food and does not properly wrap up, it is very easy to get pneumonia. I am only pointing out to Your Serene Highness that as your party has added to the number of people my servants have to wait on, I would prefer you to remain in good health."

He knew that the Princess was surprised at the way he spoke to her, but because it was good sound sense he hoped there was nothing she would do but acquiesce.

However, he had already thought out a way to save her pride, and now he said:

"I suppose I can understand to a certain extent your reluctance to accept anything, however small, from those you look on as your enemies, but I have a solution to that problem."

Although what he had said startled her she did not refute it, and the Duke continued:

"As women-servants are usually a nuisance on a yacht and more prone to sea-sickness then men, neither Lady Chatham nor Lady Radstock have brought lady's-maids with them."

He saw the Princess's eyes flicker but he went on:

"As we have been away from England for some weeks, I imagine they have quite a number of things that require mending, and I thought in return for the loan of Lady Radstock's coat and doubtless a scarf to put over your head, you could repay her by mending anything she requires while you are sitting at your father's bedside."

There was silence. Then the Princess said:

"I cannot imagine why Your Grace should ... concern yourself with ... me."

"Whether you like it or not, Your Serene Highness is my guest," the Duke said, "and because I am a perfectionist I like everything that concerns my household to run smoothly. As I have already said, your illness would be a great inconvenience."

"I have no wish to ... inconvenience you, but I will not ..."

She ceased speaking and the Duke finished the sentence by saying:

". . . accept charity from the English."

"I did not say ... that!" she exclaimed quickly.

"It is what you were thinking."

"How do ... you know what I am ... thinking?"

"For one thing, your eyes are very expressive," the Duke answered, "and for another, although I cannot explain it, I am aware that despite yourself, you are enjoying the comfort of my yacht, although resenting my being its owner."

The Princess looked distinctly startled.

He knew he had hit upon the truth and was surprised that he had been able to do so.

Then she said fiercely:

"I will not beg! It is something we have managed not to do these past six years."

"Lady Radstock told me that you worked for your food," the Duke said, "but accepting my hospitality is rather different from taking bread from those who perhaps needed it for themselves."

The Princess did not reply and he knew she was brooding over her belief that the English had been responsible for the death of the Tsar and his family.

"None of us can relive the past," he said quickly, "nor can we change what has already happened, but the future is in our hands."

He saw by the expression on her face that the future as she saw it was almost as bleak as the past had been.

She was thinking that to arrive in Egypt with her father so ill and without money was to live again the privations and the uncertainty of the past years; the only difference being that they were no longer in danger of being captured and killed by the Bolsheviks.

The Duke wanted to say that he would ensure that the future was not as frightening as she anticipated, but he knew that if he said anything of the sort she would instantly become antagonistic.

"What I am going to suggest to you," he said, "is that for the moment you forget your worries about the future and concentrate exclusively on the present. Try to enjoy yourself day by day, hour by hour, and for the moment at any rate accept an armistice between yourself and the English. You can hardly take on the whole nation single-handed."

"You are laughing at me!" the Princess said sharply.

"On the contrary, I am understanding what you feel, and I think if our roles were reversed I should feel very much the same."

His voice was stern as he said:

"Of course you are outraged that your cousins were assassinated in that cruel, brutal manner, and if they had received asylum in England they would be alive today!"

He thought she was surprised that he was so frank, but he continued:

"But you must be intelligent enough to realise that one's view of events at the time they happen may change fundamentally when the events are seen in retrospect. I am sure that at the beginning of the Revolution nobody anticipated for one moment that the Bolsheviks would gain power."

He made a gesture with his hand as he finished:

"Who would have imagined that Lenin and Trotsky would gain control of the All-Russia Congress of the Soviets and overthrow the Provisional Government."

"Even then," the Princess said in a low voice, "there was a ... chance that the Tsar and Tsarina could have been ... saved."

The Duke thought that in fact by then the British Government, even if willing, could not have negotiated with Lenin concerning the safety of the Imperial Family.

He was remembering how they had been taken to Tobolsk in Siberia, where they were imprisoned, and the following year, 1918, they were put on soldiers' rations, which put an end to all luxuries such as coffee, butter, and sugar.

Three months later they were told they would have to go on a long trip to a destination which was secret.

The Duke had heard that the journey was a nightmare of discomfort.

The Royal Family had to travel two hundred miles in the bitter cold in peasant-carts. For forty hours they moved over treacherous roads, wheels broke, and several times the horses were up to their chests in water crossing rivers.

The world outside Russia was assured that the Imperial Family were safe, but in fact the Bolsheviks, led by Lenin, had no intention of allowing the Romanovs to escape.

They were treated abominably by their new guards. These were hard-line Communists, factory-workers, who aped the behaviour of their drunken, foul-mouthed leaders.

The young Princesses were not allowed to shut their bedroom doors or to have any privacy whatsoever, and their guards made a point of taking their meals with the family in order to shock them by plunging their dirty hands into the communal dishes.

In July their duties were taken over by members of the Secret Police.

Twelve days later, the Royal Family were awakened at midnight and told that the White Army was approaching.

They were to dress quickly and come downstairs because a fleet of cars would soon be arriving to take them away.

They were assembled in a small basement room, where the Emperor and Empress were given chairs, and behind them stood the four Princesses and their brother the Tsarevich, and next to them their servants.

The Secret Police entered the room, all heavily armed.

The Tsar was killed by the first bullet, the Tsarina a second later, and in the hail of lead that followed the Princesses and their brother died quickly.

The rest of the party were all bayonetted, including the Princess Anastasia, who was only stunned when shot and then had half-a-dozen bayonets driven into her body.

The scene, which shocked the world when it was learnt what had happened, flashed through the Duke's mind, and as it did so he knew that the Princess could read his thoughts as he had read hers.

He rose from the chair on which he had been sitting and walked across the cabin to the port-hole.

He stood looking out at the sea, and he heard the Princess say behind him:

"Your country could have ... saved them."

"It is too late now," the Duke said without turning round. "But your father is alive."

"For how long?"

The Duke turned.

"I would answer that question with optimism," he said, "if I did not think that you may lessen his chance of survival by your own attitude."

He had meant to startle the Princess and he had succeeded.

"What do you mean?" she asked angrily.

"I mean," he said, "that as a Russian you are well aware that you are all extremely sensitive to other people's feelings, and their emotions, and even their thoughts. I, who am not Russian but have Scottish blood, am vividly aware of your hatred and resentment of me. Do you really believe that kind of attitude is good for your father in his present state?"

For the first time since he had known her, the Princess lost her calm and was agitated.

"I ... I do not ... understand what you are ... trying to say."

"That is not true!" the Duke retorted. "You are perfectly aware that just as I can sense your vibrations, your father is able to sense them too. What I am asking you to do is to give him hope, and that means setting aside your own personal feelings, although of course you may not love him enough to do so."

"Of course I love him!" the Princess cried. "I would die if it would make him well and prevent him from suffering as he has done these past years."

"I am not asking you to die for him, but to live

for him, and when you are as old as I am you will
find it is a much more difficult thing to do."

He saw as he spoke that the Princess was still
perturbed. Now she made a helpless little gesture with
her hands.

"As I said at the beginning of this conversation,"
he went on, "none of us can turn back the clock, but
if you love your father you will help him. I think he
needs to try to forget the tragic past by believing that
there are still many years of interesting and enjoyable
life ahead of you both."

The Duke spoke sternly. Then as if she capitulated the Princess said:

"What do you ... want me to ... do?"

"I want you to borrow the clothes you need to
make yourself less conspicuous among my guests, and
join with Prince Ivan and Prince Alexander in spending some time with us until we reach Egypt."

The Princess made an inarticulate little murmur,
but the Duke continued:

"When we arrive in Alexandria, then we will talk
together to see what can be done for your father
without making me feel that I have to climb a snow-
bound mountain if I wish to communicate with you."

There was a note of laughter in the Duke's voice
as he said the last sentence, and he thought there was
just a flicker of response in the Princess's eyes. Then
she said:

"If I ask you something ... will you tell me the
... truth?"

"Of course," the Duke replied. "As it happens, I
always speak the truth!"

"Then ... if we had just asked you to take us to
Egypt without ... demanding it in the way we did ...
would you have agreed?"

"Because I want to be completely honest with
you," the Duke answered after a moment's pause, "I
will reply that I might, if I had not realised the danger
you were in, have given you money and left you to
make your own arrangements."

He thought the Princess was about to speak, and
when she did not, he went on:

"Owing perhaps to the dramatic manner in which Prince Ivan threatened me, I was not afraid, but I became aware that you were suffering not only from starvation but from the real danger of being murdered."

"Even now I do not . . . believe that we are . . . safe," the Princess said in a low voice.

"But you are," the Duke insisted, "and that is why your attitude seems rather ridiculous when you are a guest on my yacht—and may I say very sincerely that I am delighted to have you!"

She looked at him searchingly, as if she wished to be sure this was true. Then with a little sigh she said:

"Very well, Your Grace. To prevent you from being inconvenienced by my becoming ill, I will accept the offer of Lady Radstock's coat, but, as you suggest, I will pay for the privilege by mending anything that I am given either of hers or of anybody else's."

"Pride! Pride!" the Duke said. "When Scott wrote of 'burning pride and high disdain' he might have been thinking of you!"

The Princess raised her chin.

"You may mock at pride, Your Grace, but you forget it is the only thing I have left and therefore it is very precious."

The Duke smiled.

"I understand that. At the same time, as I have already suggested, if you think of your father, pride could be harmful. What is needed is love."

He was surprised at his own words as he said them but they seemed to come to his mind.

The Princess rose to her feet and he knew she was angry.

"If you are suggesting, Your Grace, that I do not love my father and am too selfish to put my own feelings aside for him, you are very much mistaken! I would do anything . . . anything to . . . restore him to health. But I will certainly consider what you have said very carefully in case there is some truth in your assertions."

"I think you will find I am right, as I usually am," the Duke said in a lofty tone.

He thought she was about to argue with him, but instead she said:

"I think if Your Grace has now finished what you have to say, I should return to my father."

"On one condition," the Duke replied.

She waited, looking at him a little uncertainly.

"First, that you promise me that tomorow you will go out on deck," he said, "preferably about midday when the sun is at its warmest, and secondly I am hoping that when you are more settled you will join my party for meals, if not at any other time."

"May I reply that I will think about it?" the Princess answered, and moved towards the cabin door.

The Duke reached it before she did. Then, holding the handle, he said:

"You are young. Try to remember that every day of your life is precious. Enjoy the moments that are pleasant and forget the rest."

The Princess looked up at him but she could not move because he did not open the door. Then he said quietly:

"As I have said, you are young and also you are very beautiful. A great many women all over the world would be prepared to suffer a great deal for just those two precious things."

For a moment she looked at him incredulously, as if she felt she had not heard him aright.

Then she turned her face away from him to stare at the door as if she willed him to open it for her.

He opened it. Then, so swiftly that he was surprised, she had left him and vanished down the passageway.

The Duke was smiling as he went back to his cabin. He had the feeling that he had fought a complicated battle and been the victor.

Then as he settled himself comfortably in one of the armchairs to think over what had been said, the cabin door opened and Dolly came in.

"I thought you were coming back to the Saloon,

Buck," she said reproachfully, before the Duke could rise.

"I intended to do so in a few minutes."

"You have been away a long time," she said, "and I saw the Princess coming away from here just now. I suppose she has been with you?"

"I have been talking to her about her father's health."

"Was that all?"

The Duke felt irritated by her attitude.

"The Princess has been through years of misery," he said, "and in circumstances under which most women would collapse. I hope, Dolly, that you will be kind to her, for I think that all our Russian guests are greatly in need of kindness."

"I do not mind being 'kind' to her, as you call it, as long as you keep your hands off her."

It was not the way she spoke but what she said that made the Duke think, as he had never thought before, that Dolly had a common streak in her.

He always disliked it when a woman showed her jealousy too obviously.

Although it was an emotion to which he had grown accustomed, since unfortunately women always loved him more than he loved them, he knew now that he was impatient and bored with Dolly's possessive attitude.

"Do you want to stay here," he asked, "or shall we go back to the Saloon?"

"I am prepared to stay here with you, alone," Dolly replied, "and I would like you to pay me a great deal more attention than you have paid me these past twenty-four hours."

The Duke knew, by the way she spoke, that she was piqued that he had not come to her cabin last night as she had expected.

He had actually been so delighted at having rescued the Grand Duke and his party that he found that talking to the Princes with Harry and George was more attractive than she was.

They had sat up quite late, Prince Ivan fascinating

with their tales of their adventures since 1918, when
they had learnt of the assassination of the Royal Family and that the Grand Duke was on the list of those
who were also to die.

The Prince had related that they had moved from
place to place, getting poorer as the money they had
with them was spent. Then they had been forced to
sell off for very meagre sums the few jewels and other
valuables they carried with them.

"It must have been very hard on the Princess,"
Harry had remarked.

"She was magnificent!" Prince Ivan replied. "She
was only a child when we first started on our wander-
ings, but she had grown older and in circumstances
which would have made most older women faint at
the terror of it, apart from the discomfort."

"Somehow she made it an adventure," Prince
Alexander reminisced, "but you can imagine that as
she grew older and became nineteen, twenty, twenty-
one, she was always afraid that something might happen to us and she would be left alone."

"It must have been an added problem," Lord
Radstock commented.

"A very big one," Prince Ivan agreed. "There were
always men who looked at her in a way that terrified
me. Fortunately, in some ways she is still very young,
while in others she is as wise as Solomon."

The two Princes looked at each other and smiled
as if they shared a love for Militsa that was impossible
to put into words.

Then George Radstock asked them more questions and they went on talking of their adventures.

When the Duke had finally gone to his own cabin
he knew that the Princes would fall asleep the moment
their heads touched their pillows.

He had, however, lain awake for a long time going
over the tales they had told and thinking that, like
horses with an Arab strain, they had because of their
blood, their breeding, and their intelligence survived
where other men would have collapsed.

At the back of his mind he was aware that Dolly

was waiting for him, but he was less interested in her than in what he had just heard and in his own thoughts about it.

Now it suddenly struck him, almost like an iron door closing, that she no longer interested him at all.

Always before, her beauty had made him desire her physically even while many aspects of her character irritated him and he was aware that she was avaricious and greedy.

Yet when he held her in his arms nothing had seemed to matter but that she excited him and when he desired her he could forget everything else.

Now he knew that whatever attraction she had had for him, it was finished. But he told himself uncomfortably that it was an unfortunate position to be in when they were a long way from home and it was difficult to escape from each other in the yacht.

Almost as if she sensed his feelings, Dolly came and sat on the arm of his chair and put her arms round his neck.

"I love you, Buck," she said, "and I want you to love me. I resent these people intruding on our close, intimate little party because it means that they prevent us from being alone together."

The Duke forced himself to take her hand in his, but as he did so he had the unmistakable feeling he had no wish to touch her.

'I must be mad!' he thought to himself.

There had always in his varied love-affairs been a "cooling-off" period before he finally admitted that his feelings had changed and the lady in question no longer attracted him.

But never, he thought, had he known a complete "shut-down" without any warning or any time to think what he should do about it.

It flashed through his mind that perhaps he could send the whole party back from Alexandria by a different route.

There were always P. & O. ships en route from India in the harbour, on which he could book passages for them, and he thought he might say he wished to go by himself on a Safari or perhaps travel on to the Sudan.

But in the latter case he was quite sure that Dolly would insist on going with him.

"What is the matter, Buck?" she asked now. "Why are you so silent? I am worried about you."

The Duke disentangled himself from her arms and rose to his feet.

"I think I must have a cold coming," he said. "The winds are always treacherous at this time of the year."

"I certainly don't want a cold!" Dolly exclaimed. "If there is one thing that is really unbecoming it's a red nose!"

"Then you had better keep away from me."

"Perhaps I will risk it," she said after a moment's pause.

She moved towards him, but the Duke had already reached the door.

"Let us go and find the others," he said. "We don't want them to feel neglected."

"Really, Buck, I have never heard anything so ridiculous . . . !" Dolly began.

Then as the Duke was moving down the passage-way she was forced to follow him.

As she went, she thought angrily:

'It's these damned Russians who have changed everything! I wish to God they had stayed in their own country!'

Chapter Five

The Duke, watching the first rays of the sun sweeping away the darkness of the night, looked round from the bow to see that he was not the only person on deck.

Like a sportsman who sights a stag that he has been stalking for a long time, he felt an irrepressible excitement as he realised that it was Princess Militsa who was waking towards the stern.

For the last few days he had veered between frustration and anger because, despite all he had said, she had not joined the party at meals or at other times.

He knew from Nancy Radstock that she had accepted the loan of an overcoat and other small necessities in return for needlework which Nancy described as "absolutely fantastic."

"I have never seen such tiny stitches or such exquisite work," she told the Duke, "and I guessed before she told me that the Princess had been taught by a Frenchwoman who had been educated in a Convent."

The Duke smiled.

It was fashionable amongst the aristocrats in St. Petersburg to employ French Governesses and Tutors for their children, and the Tsar and his Count always spoke either in French or in English.

"At first I was only amused at her insistence on doing something for me if I lent her anything," Nancy said, "but now I am delighted when something needs mending, because she repairs it better than any shop or lady's-maid could ever do."

At least, the Duke thought, the Princess was being
sensible about that, but while he had hoped at every
meal-time she would join the party, she remained in
her father's cabin, eating with him.

Moreover, whenever he visited the Grand Duke,
which he did twice a day, she always left the cabin
and did not return until after he had gone.

This meant there was no chance of talking to her,
but he was aware before Nancy pointed it out that her
appearance was changing.

The good food, the rest, and, he thought, the
freedom from anxiety, except perhaps when she
thought about the future, had taken away the look of
strain and fear, and there was no doubt that her face
and, he suspected, her body were filling out.

'She is very beautiful,' he thought.

He found himself wondering what she would look
like dressed in the latest fashion and laughing happily
as Nancy and Dolly contrived to do even though the
latter was annoyed with him.

As he had continued to proclaim that he was
developing a cold, he had managed to avoid intimate
tête-à-têtes with Dolly, which he was certain would
end in arguments and recriminations.

Because she thought it would make him jealous,
she was indulging in an ostentatious flirtation with
Prince Alexander, who was obviously captivated by
her beauty and was only too willing to play any such
part she assigned to him.

The Duke found himself spending more time than
usual on the bridge or reading in his cabin.

He had not been surprised when Dawkins had
asked him if the Princess could borrow some of the
books he had there.

"Her Serene Highness told me she was starved of
literature," Dawkins had said, "and I told her Your
Grace could feed her with books as well as with
food."

"I am delighted for Her Serene Highness to have
anything she requires from here," the Duke had replied. "Tell her that she can come and choose them at
any time."

He hoped the Princess would do so when he was there, but he might have guessed that she was clever enough to go to his cabin when he himself was either at luncheon or at dinner

The same, he found, applied to the fresh air that he had ordered her to take.

He thought at first that she was deliberately disobeying his instructions, until he learnt that she had in fact borrowed Nancy's coat, which made him aware that she took both air and exercise at times when she was not likely to encounter him.

The Duke had never before met a woman who was determined to avoid him, just as he had never before met a woman who actively disliked him.

It made him feel strange when he thought about it, and it also gave him a challenge that he found irresistible.

He knew how grateful the Princes were for the way in which he had saved them, and the Grand Duke thanked him every time they talked together.

But Princess Militsa was made of different material.

By now he was determined to break down the barriers that she had erected and make her realise that however much she might in theory hate the English, he was different.

The difficulty was that he could find no way to talk to her.

He thought of sending Dawkins or Stevens to ask her to come to his cabin.

Then with a twist of his lips he thought that in a way that would be unsporting.

Because he was her host, she would be obliged to obey such an order. He preferred to approach her in a different maner altogether, although he was not at all certain what that should be.

He had learnt a great deal about the Princess from her father and the two Princes, especially from Prince Ivan, without their being aware that he was interested.

"As your daughter was so young when you started

out on your terrible game of 'hide-and-seek' with the
Bolsheviks," the Duke had said to the Grand Duke,
"She must have missed the education she was receiv-
ing while you were living in St. Petersburg."

He paused and added, to make his question sound
less personal:

"I was extremely impressed, when I was staying
with the Tsar, by the way Russian children, especially
girls, were more highly educated than those in any
other country in Europe."

"That is true," the Grand Duke replied, "and I
think that Militsa because she has a quick brain will
find it easy to pick up the academic learning she has
missed, while of course she has had many lessons in
life which, however bitter, must have enlarged the
horizons of her mind."

Prince Ivan confirmed this in another conversation.

"Militsa is clever," he said to the Duke. "I am sure
if she ever reaches England it will be easy for her to
get employment of some sort."

"Employment?" the Duke queried.

"Lady Radstock was telling me how since the war
women are being employed in a great number of
positions they would never have been allowed to oc-
cupy previously."

"Yes, that is true," the Duke admitted.

"I suppose," the Prince said, "that as Militsa was
so young when we went into hiding, you think her
education stopped short at what was of course a vital
age."

"I did not say so," the Duke expostulated.

"It is what everyone would think," the Prince
said, "but since the Grand Duke, as you know, is an
extremely intelligent and well-read man, and I myself
am not a complete ignoramus, I assure you that
Militsa has been learning all the time she has been
with us."

The Duke was sure that this was true, and he
realised that in consequence she was very different
from the Tsar's four daughters who had been brought

up in such a sheltered and closeted manner that they were much younger in their minds than in their years.

Interesting as the information about Princess Militsa was, it was still extremely annoying to find that he had no actual contact with her.

But now she was on deck when it was far too early for any of the rest of his party to be awake, and he moved quickly towards her in his rubber-soled yachting-shoes, making no sound on the deck.

Her back was turned and her eyes were on the green water being churned into foam behind them, though otherwise the sea was calm.

There was still a mysterious mist not yet dispersed by the sun, while in the translucent sky the last stars were fading.

The Princess was wearing Nancy's warm overcoat, and the blue chiffon scarf she had borrowed previously was draped over her head.

Her chin was lifted and she was looking back into the distance, and once again the Duke was aware of what was in her thoughts.

She was thinking of Russia, not of the Russia that had meant so much misery and privation these last years, but of the Russia she had known as a child with its wonderful Palaces filled with treasures.

The Russia of the friendship and love of the Imperial Family, and the comfort and luxury that had been so much part of her life that she had not understood how privileged she was until it was no longer there.

The Duke felt as if she told him this in words.

Then as if she sensed his presence even though he made no sound, she turned her head and saw him watching her.

For a moment they just looked at each other, then the Duke walked casually forward to join her at the rail.

"You were thinking of home?" he asked, as if they were in the midst of a conversation.

She did not pretend not to understand.

"I am being taken farther and farther away from it."

"It is no longer there," he said, "and as I told you before, it is a mistake to look back."

"I have . . . nothing now to take its . . . place," she answered.

This was so true that the Duke had no answer. They stood in silence. Then he said:

"Memories are for old people, while for you there is a whole book of blank pages waiting to be filled in."

He thought there was a faint smile on her lips as the Princess answered:

"If we could influence fate, which I do not think we can, then that would be a challenge. As it is, I can only quote Omar Khayyám:

"*'The Moving Finger writes; and, having writ,*
Moves on: nor all thy Piety nor wit
Shall lure it back to cancel half a Line.'"

The Duke laughed.

"I do not believe that is true," he said, "and I prefer:

"*'Oh threats of Hell and Hopes of Paradise!*
One thing as least is certain—This Life flies.'"

Now the Princess definitely smiled. Then she said:

"I wonder who is reading my copy of Omar Khayyám now? I loved it and drew little pictures in the margin."

"If you like poetry you will find quite a lot in my cabin."

"Yes, I know," she replied, "and it surprised me."

She obviously spoke without thinking. Then, fearing she had been rude, she said quickly:

"I am sorry. I should not have said that."

"I prefer you to speak the truth," the Duke replied. "I am well aware, although you have not said so, that you thought my Library would contain nothing but modern novels and sporting-chronicles."

She turned to look at him in surprise, and he had the feeling that her eyes looked searchingly into his, as if she was aware for the first time that he was different from what she had thought him to be.

Now he said quietly:

"You are using your perception—that insight which all Russians have."

Instantly, as if he had startled her, she replied sharply:

"Why do you say... that? And why do you behave as if you would... read my... thoughts?"

"I can read them."

"Then please... do not do so."

She turned once again to look towards the horizon and he knew that now she was not thinking of Russia but of him.

"I think you must agree," he said, "that we have a great deal in common and could talk of many things that are of interest to us both; the philosophy that is expressed in Omar Khayyám, for one."

She did not answer and after a moment he said:

> "*There was a Door to which I found no Key;*
> *There was a Veil through which I might not see:*
> *Some little talk awhile of ME and THEE.'*"

There was a distinct pause. Then the Princess said:

"My father will be waiting. I must go to him."

Without looking at the Duke she walked away, and he made no attempt to prevent her.

He only leant against the rail, thinking over their conversation and deciding it was a very strange one to have had with any woman, especially a young girl.

And yet he was aware that there were many undertones, many things they had thought without saying them aloud.

What was more, with a conviction that could not be at fault, he was certain that she could read his thoughts as easily as he could read hers.

Then once again he was irritated because she was so elusive.

"Dammit!" he exclaimed. "Why can she not show some gratitude like the rest?"

It was no consolation when at breakfast Prince Ivan exclaimed:

"I wish I could tell you, Buckminster, what it is like to sleep in the most comfortable bed I have ever known in my life and to know that I can eat everything on the table and there will still be food left over to last through the rest of the day."

He spoke as if his words came impulsively from his lips. Then as if he felt he had been somewhat unrestrained, he laughed and added:

"Forgive me. I am well aware that to a controlled Englishman I must sound very over-dramatic."

"I understand your feelings only too well," the Duke answered, "and I think it is good for all of us to listen for a change to another person's emotional reactions."

He knew that Harry looked at him in surprise, and Nancy said:

"You are right, Buck. We grow so used to complaining about our own sufferings that we forget that in other parts of the world, including Russia, there are those who, like Prince Ivan, could relate far worse experiences."

"Which is something we must not do," the Prince said, "and when I complain, tell me to shut up. But a few minutes ago I was only expressing my appreciation."

"I know that," the Duke said, "and when you have finished breakfast I thought we might walk together on deck."

"Yes, of course," the Prince agreed, knowing that the Duke wished to talk to him.

They left the Dining-Saloon after Dolly had intimated very clearly that she thought she should have been included in the invitations.

As the two men started to walk briskly round the ship, the Duke explained:

"Before we reach Alexandria I thought you and I should have a talk about your future."

"I have naturally been thinking about it," the Prince admitted. "As I told you, I have a little money in a Bank in Cairo, unless by some unfortunate chance it has been impounded."

"It should still be there," the Duke replied, "but I imagine it is not a large sum."

"No, indeed," the Prince answered. "It is some money I had in Egyptian currency when I visited Cairo in 1910. There was no need for me to have it transferred to St. Petersburg, so I left it where it was, thinking that one day it might come in useful if I visited Egypt again."

There was a smile on his lips as he added:

"It will now be very useful, as it is all I possess in the world."

"You have some friends in Egypt?"

"I believed them to be friends," the Prince replied, "but I cannot help wondering how many people who I was sure in the past cared for me for myself will find me, now that I am penniless and unimportant, both a bore and an encumbrance."

The Duke did not protest that he was sure the Prince's friends would be loyal.

He knew only too well how the aura of Royalty and wealth which had surrounded Prince Ivan in the past was very different from his present condition as a homeless White Russian.

It was debatable how many people would trouble to entertain or help him now.

The Duke had few illusions about the Social World and he had actually wondered what, if he were in similar circumstances, his own treatment would be from those who now fawned on him.

Aloud he said:

"It would be a mistake to expect too much of one's so-called 'friends.'"

"I have thought of that myself," the Prince replied, "but it is difficult to know what I can do, when, as you must be aware, I also feel responsible for the Grand Duke and Militsa."

"I suggest that for the moment you leave His Royal Highness in my hands," the Duke said.

The Prince turned to look at him and there was a sudden light in his eyes.

"Do you really mean that?"

"I promise you I will look after them both," the Duke said, "and I have a proposition to put to you which I think you might find interesting."

He knew the Prince was struggling to express his gratitude for the lifting of that burden from his shoulders, and he went on quickly:

"Since you have been out-of-touch with the news, you will not have known that last year the Tomb of one of the Pharaohs was discovered undisturbed in the Valley of the Kings opposite Luxor."

"That is interesting!" the Prince exclaimed.

"Tutankhamen, although he was quite young when he died, was buried with a wealth of treasures such as has never been unearthed before."

"How fascinating!"

"Lord Carnarvon, who financed the expedition, is a friend of mine," the Duke said, "and when I talked to him he convinced me that there must be many more Tombs as fine, if not finer, that have not been disturbed by robbers and not yet found by archaeologists."

They walked on for some minutes before the Duke said:

"I was thinking that when I visited Cairo this time I would try to find some expert in such things, with the idea that I, like Lord Carnarvon, might finance an archaeological expedition in the future."

As the Duke stopped talking he sensed the excitement rising in the Prince.

"I know very well, Your Highness," he said, "that you are a connoisseur, having seen the treasures you had in your Palace in St. Petersburg. I am interested not only in digging for treasure but also in buying antiquities which are being smuggled out of Egypt at the moment, many of which find their way to America."

"Are you suggesting," the Prince asked, "that I should do this for you?"

"If it would please you," the Duke replied. "I

cannot imagine anyone more qualified or less likely to be taken in by fakes than yourself."

"I need not tell you," the Prince said in a low voice, "what this would mean to me."

"There are also, I understand, statues, vases, and urns to be bought in Greece and in the Greek Islands, so there would be no need for you to confine yourself to Egypt."

There was a moment's silence. Then the Prince asked:

"Do you swear to me that you were really intending to find somebody to represent you in this way? You are not just creating a job for me?"

"I will swear on the Bible if necessary," the Duke replied, "that it was in my mind, and if I had not found the right person in Cairo, I might have returned home without making any decision in the matter. In which case I would undoubtedly have lost a great number of treasures which I would like to possess."

"It is difficult to say 'thank you,'" the Prince murmured.

"Then please do not try," the Duke said. "You can show your gratitude only too easily by preventing thieves from rifling the tombs and ruining them from an historical point of view."

"You may be certain that I shall let very little pass me by," the Prince said with a smile.

When their walk was finished they went down to the Duke's cabin and he wrote a letter to his Bank in Cairo, instructing them to pay the Prince a quite handsome sum as a yearly salary and also to pay any bills that he presented for his expenses or for acquisitions.

It was an arrangement in which he could very easily be defrauded, but he knew that because Prince Ivan was as proud as the Princess, he would behave with an exemplary honesty which many modern people might think absurdly conscientious.

When the letter was finished he signed it, and the Prince drew a deep breath and said:

"I cannot believe that the cloud of despondency

which has hovered over me now for seven years has been lifted."

"Forget it!" the Duke said as he had said to Militsa.

To change the subject he asked:

"Is Prince Alexander still determined to join the Foreign Legion?"

"He is looking forward to it," the Prince answered, "and quite frankly I think it will be a life to which he is admirably suited, besides improving and strengthening his character."

He thought the Duke was in agreement, and he went on:

"What is the alternative? To try to marry a rich woman? At the moment it would be difficult for Alexander to ingratiate himself into Society, having no possessions and the only clothes he has to wear being those he borrowed from you."

The Duke did not speak and the Prince finished:

"All that worries me is whether the Foreign Legion will accept him."

"That question does not arise," the Duke answered.

"Why not?"

"Because I happen to know the Commanding Officer. We fought together in the desert when he was in a junior position, and he is a Frenchman for whom I have the greatest admiration."

"So you will recommend Alexander?"

"I will certainly do that," the Duke said, "and in consequence the Prince will find no difficulty in joining the Foreign Legion, and he will be well looked after once he is a member of it."

The Prince drew in his breath.

"I am wondering now," he said in a voice charged with emotion, "why I ever doubted your generosity or imagined that you would not help us except under compulsion."

"You are safe, which is all that matters."

The Duke wondered whether, if he had been approached in an ordinary way and the Prince had come first to the yacht, he would have understood as he did now how desperately hard life had been for these aristocrats.

Their lives had been to all intents and purposes the proverbial "bed of roses" until first the war and then the Revolution had changed everything overnight.

He could not help asking himself what he would have felt if placed in similar circumstances.

Then it flashed through his mind that while he was convinced that he and Harry would have shown the same courage as the Grand Duke and the Princes, Dolly would have been very different from Militsa.

At the same time he felt hurt and disappointed that, despite everything he had said to her, the Princess still resented him and regarded him as an enemy.

He knew that the Prince was also thinking of Militsa when he said:

"There must be many Russian refugees in England by now, and if when you return you get in touch with them, I am sure that somebody amongst them would have Militsa to live with them."

"I have thought of that," the Duke replied, "and as I have already told you, I will look after both the Grand Duke and the Princess."

"Perhaps you could find her a husband," the Prince said, as if he was following his own train of thought. "I am sure that if she was properly dressed, men would find her attractive."

"I am sure they would."

"Because she has never been in the company of men except for Alexander and myself," the Prince went on, "she has no idea how to flirt or how to charm a man, but when the opportunity arises I suppose that sort of thing comes naturally to a woman!"

"I expect it does," the Duke agreed. "But I have very little experience of young girls."

The Prince gave a little laugh.

"I could say the same! The women who attracted me in the old days were all beauties so sophisticated and so polished that they shone as dazzling as the jewels they wore round their necks and on their heads."

He threw out his hands as he said:

"Do you remember how exquisite the women looked at that last Ball you attended at the Winter Palace?"

"I shall never forget it."

"I was very much in love with a lovely woman whose husband was fortunately away on Army manoeuvres. We danced together and when I took her home I think I was happier that night than I have ever been in my whole life."

He sighed.

"I used to think about her when I was sleeping under a hay-stack or moving at night from a village where they were making too many enquiries about us to another. I wonder where she is now."

The Duke though it very likely that she had died as so many other Russian aristocrats had done, but there was no point in saying so, and he merely replied:

"Perhaps one day you will find her again. Many escaped, and I am sure there is a whole colony of them in Cairo as there is in London and in Paris."

The Prince shook his head.

"There would be no point in searching—how do you say?—for a 'needle in a hay-stack.' Memories should remain unspoilt and I could not bear to be disillusioned."

"It is something that happens far too often," the Duke said cynically.

"Of course, and that is life," the Prince agreed.

Then, as if he had no wish to think of himself, he said:

"I am deeply grateful and very relieved that you will look after Militsa. She has not yet been disillusioned about love, whatever she has suffered in other ways."

"Then let us hope that such a condition is not inevitable," the Duke said.

He spoke lightly but the Prince was frowning.

"Militsa is still young in years," he said, "and you may not understand, but in the Orient they believe in the Wheel of Rebirth. If that is true, then she is one of those who have been born many times before."

It struck the Duke that this was what he himself believed but had never put it into words.

"I have studied Buddhism," he replied, "and found it very interesting, especially the Theory of Reincarnation."

"There is no other explanation," the Prince said, "for the fact that sometimes people we meet for the first time can seem so familiar that they are already a part of ourselves."

He saw that the Duke was listening, and he went on:

"Also how else can you explain the extraordinary talent of children who hardly know their alphabet and yet like Mozart can compose a Concerto at age six?"

"When I was in India," the Duke said, "I accepted the Theory of Rebirth because it seemed unanswerable. But when I returned to the more mundane atmosphere of England, I doubted my own credulity."

"At least after my experiences in this incarnation," the Prince said, "I should be rewarded with a far more comfortable life in the next!"

He spoke lightly and the seriousness of what they had been saying was swept away.

Yet later that day the Duke thought of it again.

He visited the Grand Duke before luncheon, and as if the Princess had anticipated what time he would do so, she was not in her father's cabin when the Duke entered it.

"How are you, Sir?" he asked the Grand Duke.

"I have had a little pain during the night, but otherwise I cannot complain. And I want to thank you for your great kindness to Ivan. He has told me what you have offered him and it has made me very happy."

"I am glad about that."

"I must tell you how kind he has been to me," the Grand Duke continued. "I was a heavy encumbrance on those young people, so much so that I often thought the sooner I died the better!"

"That would have been a very inconsiderate thing to do!" the Duke exclaimed, and as the Grand Duke saw that he was determined not to be serious, he laughed.

"Now that you have arranged Ivan's and Alexander's futures," he said, "it only remains for Militsa and me not to be a nuisance and outstay our welcome."

"You will never do that, Sir," the Duke said quickly.

"I thought that as soon as I am well again," the Grand Duke went on, "I might try to write a book. It is something I have never done before, but I was always very fluent in my speeches and the Tsar told me that when I described anything to him I painted a picture."

"I think that would be an excellent idea!" the Duke approved. "I feel that Your Royal Highness's memoirs would have great historic value. After all, you know things of which most other people are not aware, even if they lived in Court Circles."

"That is true," the Grand Duke said, "and therefore I must get to work quickly. Do you think my book would make money?"

"I am quite certain it would," the Duke replied.

They talked about many of the events and scenes he could describe, and when he saw that the Grand Duke was beginning to tire, the Duke left him.

As he went from the cabin he wondered if he should knock on Militsa's door and insist on speaking to her.

Then he told himself angrily that if she wished to go on hating him like a child, he would merely ignore her.

It was absurd to let one young woman annoy him and invade his thoughts.

But during luncheon it was impossible for him not to keep thinking that the Princess was below and had no intention of joining them.

As if Dolly had suddenly realised that she was losing his interest, she made special efforts to hold his attention and to show, by her words and the caressing movements of her hands, that she loved him.

The Duke knew that a week ago he would have responded ardently for no other reason than that she was so beautiful. So it was easy to understand why Prince Alexander found it impossible to take his eyes from her.

Yet now it was a relief to talk to Nancy, who was on his other side, and she made him laugh as she always did.

At the same time, he told himself, that she was a kind woman and that, strangely enough in the somewhat raffish society in which they moved, he was sure she was completely faithful to her husband.

"What are we going to do this afternoon?" Nancy asked.

Before the Duke could reply, Dolly answered:

"What can we do except try to fill out the hours on this boring boat, while Buck stares at the sea as if he were Moses or whoever it was who parted the waves!"

They all laughed and Dolly went on:

"If you ask me, I think it's a crashing bore that we have to rush to Alexandria instead of stopping at other places on the way. I am sure there are things we could buy en route if we looked for them."

"I doubt it," the Duke replied. "Do you ever think of anything but shopping?"

"Not when I have you with me, sweetie!" Dolly replied. "Anyway, what else could be more amusing, except one thing which I am too discreet to say out loud?"

They laughed again, and then Prince Alexander was teasing her, and what the Duke felt might have been an uncomfortable moment passed.

He spent the afternoon, as Dolly had predicted, on the bridge, looking at the sea, and he became all the more determined to talk to the Princess.

He therefore went down an hour earlier than usual to call on the Grand Duke.

The cabin door was closed and he was just about

to knock when the door next to it opened and the
Princess stood there.

"My father is asleep."

"I am rather earlier than usual," the Duke replied, "because I wanted to talk to you."

"Why?"

"We did not finish our conversation this morning."

"I am finished. There is nothing more to say."

"On the contrary, there is a great deal more," the
Duke persisted, "and as your father does not require
your services, I suggest you come to my cabin. If you
have no wish to talk about yourself, we can at least
discuss poetry."

"I am resting," the Princess said.

"That is not true, because I can see that you are
sewing," he answered.

The Duke looked past her to where on the bed
lay a blouse belonging to Nancy, which he was sure
she had been stitching when she heard his footsteps
outside the door.

She looked indecisive and he said:

"If you prefer, I can of course talk to you in
here."

He thought there was a faint flush in her cheeks,
as if she realised that that would be unconventional,
and she said quickly:

"No, I will come to your cabin, but I cannot stay
long. Papa should wake soon."

"Dawkins will not be far away," the Duke answered consolingly.

He walked ahead of her as he had done before.
When they entered his cabin and he shut the door,
he had a distinct feeling of triumph, as if he had captured some rare wild bird and taken it into captivity.

Because she had no wish to meet his eyes, the
Princess was staring at the bookcase which covered
one wall of the cabin.

"Are you approving my taste?" the Duke enquired.

"Your books make me feel very ignorant," she replied. "I find myself wishing, as I have a thousand times these last years, that I had studied harder when I had the chance."

"To what end?" the Duke enquired.

She looked at him in surprise. Then she asked:

"Surely you are not questioning my desire for knowledge or suggesting that a woman should be just an empty-headed play-thing to amuse men?"

The remark was so unexpected that the Duke threw back his head and laughed.

"Where can you have got such ideas?" he asked.

"It was actually Lady Radstock who warned me against being too clever," the Princess replied. "She said men are afraid of clever women and all they want is that they should look pretty and dance well."

"It should not be difficult for you to achieve such a grand ambition," the Duke remarked sarcastically.

The Princess made a sound of derision.

"I have no intention of wasting my time on anything so foolish," she said. "I intend to find employment of some sort, so I must improve my mind. Fortunately, I can speak several languages."

"What have you considered doing?"

"I understand nowadays women work in all sorts of different ways," the Princess answered. "Lady Radstock thought it might be possible for me to obtain a position in an Embassy."

There was a pause. Then the Princess said in a low voice:

"She said if I wanted to do...that, I would... need your...help."

"So you are beginning to find I can be useful."

"Lady Radstock said that you know a great number of people in Cairo."

The Duke was about to say that he intended taking both her and the Grand Duke back to England, but he felt, knowing what she thought about his country, that she might immediately begin to argue.

He therefore said nothing, and the Princess,

turning back to the books, took out first one, then
another, before she said:

"I think you will have to help me. I want a book
that will tell me how I should behave in the modern
world, of which I know nothing."

She turned towards the Duke as she said:

"I am aware that there is an enormous gap not
only in my life but also in my mind, between the
world I left in 1917 and the world to which I have
returned in 1924. What knowledge do I need to fill
those years?"

"I think you will find it easier to do as Lady
Radstock suggested—look pretty and dance well!"

The Duke meant to tease her, but the anger that
flashed into her eyes made her, he thought, look even
more beautiful than she had before.

She was no longer a statue, proud and aloof.
Instead she was a very human woman, emotional
and easily upset.

"What you are suggesting is ridiculous and in
my opinion degrading!"

She pulled out of the bookcase the first book that
came to her hand, and without looking again at the
Duke walked out of the cabin.

He was sure that if she had been wearing a
dress made of silk with a full skirt, she would posi-
tively have flounced as she left.

The Duke did not move.

He merely lay back in his chair, and he was
smiling as he thought over what had just occurred.

Chapter Six

The Duke looked at his watch. It was not yét twelve o'clock, which was the time he had instructed a Doctor, by radio-telegraph, to call on the yacht.

They had, however, docked earlier than expected and quite a lot had happened since then.

First, Prince Ivan had discovered that the fastest train to Cairo left at eleven and the Duke had suggested that he and Prince Alexander should be on it.

"As soon as I know the Grand Duke's condition," he had said, "and if he has to go into Hospital, which I think likely, it will take at least twenty-four hours to make arrangements for a private sleeping-carriage."

"We could wait and come with you," Prince Ivan had replied.

The Duke shook his head.

"That is unnecessary, and I think it would be useful for you to begin making enquiries about our joint venture as soon as possible. If you have any information for me when we arrive, it would make it easier for us to discuss our plans for the future."

Prince Ivan saw the sense of this, and as Prince Alexander, delighted with the Duke's introduction to the Officer in Command of the Foreign Legion, was anxious to present it, he decided to go with him.

They said good-bye to the Grand Duke and Militsa, who had breakfasted as usual in their cabin. Dolly had done the same, so the Duke had not seen her this morning.

He had lain awake most of the night, wondering what he should do about her.

It was impossible for him to leave the party as he might otherwise have done, since the responsibility for the Grand Duke and the Princess rested entirely on him.

He heard someone coming up the gangplank and looked round, hoping it might be the doctor, only to see instead an Egyptian carrying a parcel.

Because he was curious, he walked to where the man was discussing what he had brought with the steward on duty, and heard him say:

"For—Princess! Gentleman say—just for lady—called Princess."

"Take it to Her Serene Highness," the Duke said to the steward.

Then, because he was curious, he asked the Egyptian:

"What does your parcel contain?"

"Very nice dress, Sir. From best shop in—town. You—visit?"

He pulled a card from his robe as he spoke and pressed it into the Duke's hand.

He took it, and he was thinking that he understood now the reason why Prince Ivan had hurried from the yacht earlier than he thought necessary to reach the station.

They had never discussed it, but the Duke was sure Prince Ivan knew why she had continued to wear her ragged, threadbare gown and refused to accept anything but the loan of absolute necessities from the hated English.

He wondered now, if she was dressed in a gown which was her own, whether she would condescend to join him and the rest of the party at meals.

He thought it would be interesting to see her reaction. He also thought that he might go below and enquire how the Grand Duke was this morning.

He was just about to do so when he was aware that the Egyptian had left and another man was climbing the gangplank.

He thought it must be the Doctor, and as he waited to greet him Dolly came to his side.

"Here you are, Buck," she said. "Why did nobody tell me that Prince Ivan and Alexander were leaving so early?"

"They asked me to say good-bye to you," the Duke replied, "and to thank you for making the voyage from Constantinople so very enjoyable."

"I shall miss them," Dolly said. "At the same time, I much prefer to be alone with . . ."

She broke off what she was saying and gave a sudden scream as the man the Duke had seen climbing the gangplank was suddenly standing beside them.

The Duke looked up and exclaimed:

"Robert! What are you doing here?"

"Hello, Buck," the Earl of Chatham replied.

He bent to kiss his wife on the cheek.

"I thought you would be surprised to see me, Dolly!"

"I am," Dolly answered. "I imagined you miles away chasing lions—or should I say 'lionesses'?"

She spoke in the light, frivolous manner she always used to her husband, but the Earl's voice was serious as he said quietly:

"I received a telegram telling me that I should return home immediately as my mother is dying."

"I am sorry," the Duke said.

"I was trying to find out where you were so that I could inform Dolly that she must join me, when I learnt *The Siren* had docked early this morning."

"I was not expecting to be here so soon," the Duke replied.

"I have been waiting until you arrived," the Earl went on, "because Dolly can now travel home with me."

He looked at his wife as he spoke, and both he and the Duke were aware that Dolly wished to protest that she had no wish to leave the yacht.

She knew, however, that it would be an insult to her mother-in-law if she continued to holiday in the Mediterranean when it was possible for her husband to return from Africa.

"Is there really so much hurry?" she asked.

"I doubt if by the time we arrive home Mother will be alive," the Earl answered.

"What are your plans?" the Duke asked, as Dolly did not speak.

"I have booked two cabins on a P. & O. Steamer which is leaving this afternoon," the Earl said, "and it will be quicker if we get off at Rome and go on by train."

"I loathe trains!" Dolly said crossly.

The Duke knew what she really loathed was having to leave him, but he could not help feeling an irrepressible relief that he was to be rid of her.

"I am sorry about all this, Robert," he said to the Earl. "Come into the Saloon and have a drink."

"I would like some coffee," the Earl answered. "It is too early for anything else."

"I agree with you," the Duke said.

He was just about to move from the gangway when he saw the man for whom he had been waiting get out of an aged, rather ramshackle car.

Despite his tropical suit he looked exactly as a Doctor should and was even carrying the traditional black bag.

The Duke turned to Dolly.

"Here is the Doctor to see the Grand Duke. Look after your husband; and I am sure he will want to see Nancy and George."

He did not wait for her to reply but greeted the Doctor as he stepped aboard and took him down to the Grand Duke's cabin.

It was half-an-hour later that Dawkins brought the Doctor to the Duke's own cabin.

He had not joined the rest of his party because for one thing he was nervous in case Dolly should try to make excuses to remain on the yacht and let her husband travel home alone, and for another because he was genuinely anxious as to what verdict the Doctor would give on the Grand Duke's condition.

The Duke thought, although he might have been mistaken, that His Royal Highness had seemed weaker in the last forty-eight hours.

Dawkins had reported that he had spasms of pain especially at night, and the Duke had known it was imperative for him to have a medical opinion as quickly as possible.

Now as the Doctor, who was English, came into the cabin, the Duke was aware that his expression was grave.

"Will you sit down, Dr. Johnson?" the Duke asked. "You will naturally understand that I am very anxious to have your verdict on my guest's health."

They had all decided that before they reached Cairo it would be a mistake to tell anyone of the Grand Duke's true identity.

That he was a friend of the Duke's would be enough introduction for him to have the best treatment in any Hospital, and although they believed that they were now safe from the vengeance of the Bolsheviks, there was no point in proclaiming that an aristocrat who they had announced as being dead had in fact survived.

It was Prince Ivan who had suggested that he should be referred to as Count Alexis Dubenski.

"I think there were a million Counts in Russia before the war," he said, "and Dubenski is quite a common name."

Dr. Johnson took off his glasses and polished them reflectively before he said:

"I am afraid, Your Grace, I have no good news to give you about your friend Count Alexis."

"I rather anticipated that," the Duke replied.

"He has a growth in his intestines which I suspect is cancer. But even if it is not, he will require a major and serious operation."

The Duke sighed. Then he said:

"Is there a Surgeon either in Alexandria or Cairo you could recommend?"

The Doctor paused for a moment before he said:

"If I am to answer that question frankly, then the answer is 'no.' But there is in fact one man, Your

Grace, who, if the Count's condition is as serious as
I think, is capable of saving his life."

"Who is that?" the Duke enquired.

"He is called Schmidt. He is Swiss and has a
Hospital in Monte Carlo. He specialises in this particular branch of surgery and is, I believe, a genius
in his own field."

"Then the best thing I can do," the Duke said,
"is to take the Count to Monte Carlo as quickly as
possible."

"I must impress upon you, Your Grace, that time
is always a vital factor in conditions like this, and
the Count is already in an extremely weak state of
health."

Dr. Johnson told the Duke that he had given
Dawkins certain medicines that would relieve the
pain and prescribed others which might help him.

"Your man has already gone ashore to the Chem-
ist," he finished.

The Duke thanked him, paid him for his services,
and escorted him to the gangway.

"This is a very beautiful yacht," Dr. Johnson
said, looking round. "At least your friend will travel
more comfortably to Monte Carlo than he might have
done otherwise."

"That is true," the Duke agreed. "But I wish you
could have given me a happier report on his condition."

"So do I," the Doctor replied, "but may I say,
Your Grace, it has been a very great pleasure to meet
you. I remember reading of your exploits during the
war and how excited we used to be when you pulled
off one coup after another with your armoured cars."

The Duke smiled.

"It seems a very long time ago now."

"All the same, some of us do not forget," the
Doctor replied.

He shook the Duke's hand effusively before he
drove away in his ancient car.

The Duke went to the Saloon and found to his
surprise that only Nancy was there.

She jumped up when he appeared, saying:

"I was waiting for you, Buck. I want to tell you something."

"What is it?"

"I don't want you to be offended, but I feel that if Dolly has to go home, I ought to go with her."

The Duke raised his eye-brows and Nancy explained:

"She is going to be difficult about leaving you, and both George and I feel that as she is so impulsive, she might alienate Robert completely and break up their marriage."

She saw the surprise in the Duke's expression, and she added:

"Please do not think I am prying into your affairs, but I do not think you want to marry Dolly."

"Marry her? No, of course not!"

The Duke was so astonished that the words seemed to ejaculate from his lips.

"But I am sure that is what Dolly intends," Nancy said. "I thought, however, although I may be mistaken, that these last few days you were not so infatuated with her as you were."

The Duke was not surprised that Nancy was perceptive where he was concerned.

She and her husband had been close friends of his for so long that they had seen him pass through quite a number of love-affairs. Now he realised that the fact that he had suddenly found that Dolly no longer attracted him had been obvious to Nancy if not to her.

"She cannot really expect me to want to marry her," he said, feeling that such an idea was incredible. "Anyway, I thought in her own way she was quite fond of Robert."

"Dolly wants to be a Duchess," Nancy said simply.

"And wear the Buckminster jewels," the Duke finished in a low voice, as if he spoke to himself.

Now he understood a great many things Dolly had said which at the time had not alerted him to the fact that she was hoping to become his wife rather than remain his mistress.

"I suppose it is my fault," he said, "but Robert did not seem to mind."

"Robert is fed up with the way Dolly treats him," Nancy replied, "but I think if you were not available she would realise on which side her 'bread is buttered' and would make herself more pleasant."

"I certainly hope so!" the Duke exclaimed.

"At the same time," Nancy continued, "we both know how impulsive Dolly is, and I think I should be there to safe-guard not only her interests but—yours."

The Duke understood exactly what Nancy was saying.

In a fit of pique or anything else which upset her, Dolly might go so far as to demand a divorce, and in the circumstances Robert might agree to give it to her.

The Duke knew there was nothing he would dislike more than being married to Dolly, with her moods, her insatiable greed, and her very limited conversation.

It struck him for perhaps the first time that women should have something else to talk about besides love, and other interests besides dancing.

Aloud he said:

"You are a good friend, Nancy, and I am extremely grateful to you and George. I know you will neither of you be offended if, because I brought you on this trip, you will remain my guests until you are actually back in England."

Nancy moved nearer to him to slip her arm through his.

"Thank you, Buck," she said. "I am not going to pretend that we do not need the money or that it is not hard to make ends meet, especially when all our friends are so much richer than we are."

"I owe you a great deal more than mere money," the Duke replied.

"I will go now," Nancy said, "and I will tell George and Harry they can join you. They knew I wanted to see you alone."

"Wait a moment," the Duke said as she turned away. "I have to see the Princess and her father. Tell

Harry that we are leaving immediately for Monte Carlo."

"Monte Carlo?" Nancy asked questioningly.

"The Grand Duke has to have an operation and the only man capable of doing it is a Dr. Schmidt."

"I have heard of him!" Nancy exclaimed. "He is brilliant! I am sure the Grand Duke will recover in his hands."

"That is what I hope," the Duke said, "but now I have to tell the Princess how ill her father is."

"I am sorry. She will be very upset," Nancy replied. "She adores him, and if he dies, what on earth will happen to her?"

"We will cross that bridge when we come to it," the Duke answered. "The main thing at the moment is to keep him alive."

"Yes, of course," Nancy agreed, "but if, on the other hand, she is left alone in the world, I will do my best to help her."

"Thank you, Nancy, and mind you tell her that before you leave."

"I will," Nancy replied.

The Duke went below, aware as he walked towards the Grand Duke's cabin that he could hear Dolly's voice raised in her own cabin, and he knew that she was quarrelling with her husband.

He realised that he had had a very lucky escape, but he could not help being apprehensive until two hours later when the Chathams and the Radstocks had left the yacht.

The Captain was getting up steam while waiting for the last consignment of fresh food that had been ordered by Stevens to come aboard.

Now that most of the original guests with whom he had started the voyage had gone, the Duke was not surprised to find Harry waiting for him when he left the Grand Duke's cabin.

"I want to talk to you a moment, Buck," he said.

"I seem to have been doing nothing but talking the whole morning!" the Duke exclaimed. "I hoped I would have a little peace this afternoon."

"You may get that in the next world but certainly not in this," Harry said with a smile.

The Duke took out his watch.

"We will be leaving in about twenty minutes, so if you have a lot to say it had better wait until after we have started."

"It will not take long," Harry said. "I am just hoping you will not be annoyed if I stay in Cairo for a few days and rejoin you after you have reached Monte Carlo."

"I am not annoyed," the Duke replied, "but I am curious."

"I thought you would be," Harry smiled, "but the truth is that when I knew you intended to visit Cairo, I wrote to an old flame of mine—someone who meant a great deal to me when we were here during the war—and told her I would call on her as soon as we arrived."

"I know who you are talking about!" the Duke exclaimed. "Go on!"

"She wrote back very enthusiastically, and quite frankly I was looking forward to seeing her again."

"Then of course neither you nor she should be disappointed," the Duke said.

"I thought you would understand," Harry remarked.

"You thought nothing of the sort," the Duke retorted, "so why not be truthful?"

Harry laughed.

"You always could detect when I was lying. Well, to be honest, I was a little apprehensive because I know you hate your plans being changed, but as you will have quite enough to do looking after the Grand Duke and of course Princess Militsa, I will not feel as guilty as I might otherwise have done!"

"Go and enjoy yourself," the Duke laughed, "and don't hurry unnecessarily to join me. I expect to be staying in Monte Carlo for some time."

"Will you open your Villa?"

"Yes, of course. I am sending a telegram today warning them of my arrival."

"There will certainly be a lot of your friends in Monte Carlo to welcome you," Harry said, "and you might be able to persuade the Princess to come out of 'purdah'!"

"I might," the Duke agreed.

There was a note in his voice that made Harry smile secretly to himself.

He knew the Duke too well and was too fond of him not to be aware that there was some connection between the ending of his love-affair with Dolly and his interest in the Princess.

He did not think that at the moment she attracted him as a woman, but that he was intrigued by her attitude just as he had been intrigued and excited by the drama they had encountered in Constantinople when Prince Ivan had demanded his help.

The Duke had awakened, Harry thought, and was being lifted out of the boredom that had enveloped him since the end of the war.

He seemed more alert and was using his brain in a way he had not had to do for some years.

He was well aware that the Duke was at his best when planning other people's lives or solving the complications of his own.

He was a born leader; a man who was meant to be a campaigner in one way or another. Harry knew that he would fight to keep the Grand Duke alive, and also in a more personal way to make the Princess conform to the behaviour he expected of her.

'It is not going to be easy for him to get his own way,' Harry thought to himself, 'and that is the best thing that could possibly happen where Buck is concerned.'

At luncheon he knew that the Duke's high spirits, the way he joked with both the Earl and George, arose from the pleasure of knowing that Dolly was leaving and he could metaphorically "clear the decks" for his new preoccupation.

Because Harry was so fond of the Duke, he wished he knew Militsa well enough to tell her to go on fighting him and being difficult.

Then he thought he was being foolish.

"She is too young," he told him, "but because
her pride is different from anything Buck has ever
come in contact with before, she will keep him guess-
ing until they reach Monte Carlo."

Doubtless after that, he thought, the "hangers-on"
would be waiting to swarm over the Duke and draw
him back into the fold.

He was always very cynical about those who
forced themselves upon the Duke simply because he
was rich, but at least, he thought, Militsa was not
amongst them, and he wondered how long she would
keep refusing everything he offered because he was
English.

He thought of the emeralds that Dolly had been
expecting to be given in Cairo and knew that that
was another reason why she would make herself unpleasant to her husband.

He thought now that he had never really liked
her. Although she was undoubtedly one of the most
beautiful women he had ever seen, there was something repulsive about her greed. She was in fact the
epitome of what the Americans so aptly called a
"gold-digger."

"Buck can do better than that," Harry told himself.

He looked at him and thought that because he
was so good-looking, so rich, and above all a Duke,
it would be very difficult for him to be loved for
himself.

It struck him that what was missing in the Duke's
life, and what he really wanted, was the love that
came from the heart and had nothing to do with the
wealth and other advantages with which he was so
well endowed.

Harry guessed that when Dolly had managed to
get the Duke alone for one moment before they left,
she would make a last effort to hold on to him.

"Will you miss me, Buck?" she asked as Robert
carried her jewel-case down the gangplank towards
the car that was waiting to take them to the P. & O.
Liner.

"Of course," he replied.

"I shall be thinking about that lovely time we might have had together in Cairo."

Dolly's voice was very caressing. Then as the Duke did not respond she went on:

"If Robert's mother is not as ill as he anticipates, I will join you in Monte Carlo."

The Duke tried to find words in which to say that this was something he did not want, but at that moment the Earl returned, saying:

"Come on, Dolly! You know we must get aboard as quickly as possible and find some decent accommodation for Nancy and George."

"Oh, don't fuss!" Dolly replied. "I'm coming! Good-bye, Buck!"

She lifted her face to the Duke's, and he kissed her cheek and held out his hand to the Earl.

"Good-bye, Robert," he said, "and I hope by the time you reach England your mother will have taken a turn for the better."

"So do I," the Earl replied.

Then they had gone and the Duke went back inside. Now Harry said with a smile:

"My trunks are nearly empty—the Princes have made a large hole in my wardrobe!"

"And in mine," the Duke replied, "but they could hardly appear in Cairo looking as they did when we first saw them."

Harry laughed.

"That is true, and I don't begrudge them my clothes, except that I wanted to look my best for the next few days."

"You are fishing for compliments," the Duke said accusingly. "She is seven years older than when you last saw her and doubtless she will think you look it."

"In which case I shall be joining you in Monte Carlo within the next twenty-four hours!"

"You know I shall be glad to see you," the Duke replied.

After Harry had left, the yacht began to move.

As the Duke went to the bridge to see them steam out of the harbour, he thought he had never expected to spend such a very short visit in Egypt.

Now with his party dispersed he was left with only a very ill old man and a girl who had no wish to talk to him.

It struck the Duke that this was his opportunity to make her do so.

Whatever other plans had been changed, the challenge Militsa offered him was still there.

He thought of how he had accused her of having a "burning pride" and how she had said it was the only thing she had left.

'How can I convince her,' he thought, 'that there are many other things in the world and that pride can be a very poor substitute for friendship and of course—love?'

The word surprised him and he recalled how Prince Ivan had said that perhaps he would be able to find her a husband.

"There will be plenty of men in Monte Carlo who will find her attractive," he told himself.

As she disliked the English so much, he wondered what other nationalities would gain her approval.

The Siren was steering a course between a number of small boats, their sails billowing out in the wind.

The sea was very blue and in the sunshine everything seemed to have a golden glimmer about it.

'The Princess should look at this,' the Duke thought, and again he felt irritated by the way she made herself so inaccessible.

" 'A burning pride and high disdain,' " he quoted to himself, and thought that nothing could describe her better.

But that was all a lot of nonsense, he thought, for someone so young and inexperienced.

"Dammit all! I will make her obey me!" he vowed.

He was so long on the bridge that when he finally left it, the sun had lost its warmth.

The Duke went inside and was just thinking that it was time for him to call on the Grand Duke when Dawkins appeared to say:

"Her Serene Highness wishes to speak to you in your cabin, Your Grace."

"I will go there at once," the Duke replied. "Is His Royal Highness awake?"

"No, Your Grace. He is asleep, and I think the Doctor's medicine helped, as he was in a bit of pain before he drank it."

"Then let him sleep as much as he can," the Duke said. "I have told the Captain to get us to Monte Carlo as quickly as possible."

He moved away as he spoke, wondering what Militsa had to say to him.

When he had told her father that he had to have an operation and the best man to do it was in Monte Carlo, the Grand Duke had acepted it quite philosophically, but Militsa had become very pale and had clasped her hands together.

She had said nothing, and the Duke had gone on:

"I am told Dr. Schmidt is brilliant, especially at the kind of surgery that your father needs. And I happen to know he has a modern, well-equipped Hospital in Monte Carlo with every comfort."

"I am sorry you have had to change your plans," the Grand Duke said. "It is very gracious of you."

He spoke with the old-world courtesy that had given him an unmistakable charm in the old days.

"Quite frankly," the Duke answered, "I do not mind missing Cairo, which I have always thought is a noisy place, and I know that Prince Ivan will represent my interests as well as, if not better than, I could do myself."

"He is very grateful for your kindness, as I am for what you have done for Alexander," the Grand Duke said.

"Now, all that is important," the Duke replied, "is to get you into the hands of Dr. Schmidt, and we will start as soon as our provisions are aboard."

The Grand Duke smiled.

"I certainly would not wish you to leave those behind!"

Now as he waited for the Princess in his cabin, the Duke remembered that while her father had thanked

him again when he left the cabin, she had said
nothing.

He had glanced at her and her eyes had seemed
very large and dark in her pale face. He had thought
that it was due to the shock of knowing her father
had to have an operation and that it was rather foolish
of him to have expected anything else.

The door opened.

"Her Serene Highness, Your Grace!" Dawkins
said.

She came in and the Duke saw that she was different and it took him a second to realise why.

For the first time since he had met her she was
wearing a light-coloured dress, and he knew that it
was the one that Prince Ivan had bought for her before he caught the train.

It was a very simple gown of a thin muslin that
women wore in the tropics, and it had obviously been
a cheap purchase in one of the many small cave-like
shops that were situated by the docks.

The dress was of a flowered material on a white
background, and although it was a little too large for
the Princess it was at least a fashionable length, reaching just above the ankles. The Duke realised that for
the first time she was wearing stockings, which the
Prince must also have bought.

He could see now that she had slim, elegant
ankles, but she was still wearing the battered slippers that she had worn ever since she came on board.

Nevertheless, she looked very different without
her threadbare gown and the red table-cloth that had
kept her warm until they reached the sun of Egypt.

In fact, the Duke thought, the pale colour of her
dress made her look more beautiful than she had
before and certainly much younger.

It seemed to lighten her skin, her hair, and even
her eyes, but he was aware as soon as he looked at
her that she was troubled about something, and he
thought that if she was apprehensive about her father's
operation, which indeed she had every reason to be, he
must somehow try to reassure her.

"I want to ... speak to ... you," the Princess said.

Now it struck him that she was talking in a different voice, shy and a little hesitating, which was quite unlike the aloof, imperious tone in which she had addressed him in the past.

"I am delighted that you should wish to do so," the Duke replied. "Shall we sit down?"

He indicated the chair in which she had sat once before when he had known that she was hiding the fact that she was wearing no stockings.

He seated himself opposite her and waited.

Because she had been so difficult up until now, he saw no reason to make it easy for her or even to try to anticipate what she had to say.

"I . . . I do not know how to . . . begin," she said a little helplessly.

"If you are going to express your gratitude," the Duke said, "may I point out that your father has been very eloquent on the subject, and quite frankly I do not like being thanked."

"I do not think that is true," the Princess replied, as if she felt she must argue. "Everybody likes appreciation."

The Duke smiled.

"Very well, I will listen to you if all you wish to say is 'thank you.'"

"I do thank you," the Princess said, "but that . . . is not all."

The Duke was puzzled.

"I am of course more grateful," she went on, "than I can ever put into words that you will not only give up your plans of visiting Cairo to take Papa to Monte Carlo, but that you will also . . . pay for his . . . operation."

The last words came out in a sudden rush, and now the Duke knew why she had to see him and why she was embarrassed and shy.

"I am pleased to do anything within my power to help your father," he said.

"That is . . . not the point."

"Then what is?"

Again there was a hesitation, and now she looked

down, her eye-lashes very dark against her pale
cheeks.

"I am ... wondering how I can ... repay you."

It was what he might have expected, the Duke
thought.

It had in fact never struck him that Militsa, who
had mended Nancy's clothes all the way to Alexandria,
would still feel it incumbent upon herself to pay what
would undoubtedly be a very large sum for her father's
operation.

The Duke knew that in Monte Carlo of all places
any Doctor would expect a Harley Street fee or even
double.

However, what it would cost was quite immaterial
to him, and now as he realised what was worrying
Militsa he thought it would be interesting to know
in what way she proposed to repay him for his
generosity.

She was waiting for his answer, and he said:

"You can hardly be expected to be responsible for
your father's debts."

"But ... I must stay with him," the Princess said
sharply.

"Of course," the Duke agreed.

"And that will cost you money."

"Naturally."

There was silence. Then she said:

"I ... I know that you ... dislike my p-pride ...
but it is something which is ... born in me."

"That we have already established," the Duke
answered, "but in this instance you will have to bury
your pride, however unpleasant you may find it, and
accept my charity, if that is what you wish to call it."

He was being provocative and he wondered if
her eyes would flash at him as they had before.

But she still looked down at her hands in her lap,
and he thought as he followed her gaze how long, thin,
and aristocratic her fingers were and how shapely the
hands themselves.

"I have ... something to ... suggest," the Princess
said at length in a voice that was barely audible.

"I am curious to know what your suggestion will be," the Duke replied.

It flashed through his mind that perhaps she wanted to give him an I.O.U. for the future when she had found employment as she intended.

He thought a little mockingly that if she had to earn what she and her father would cost him in one way and another, it would certainly take her a long time to refund it.

Then he was aware that the Princess was finding it difficult to put into words what she was thinking.

For the first time he knew that she was very tense and even trembling a little.

In the same impersonal voice in which he had spoken to her before, he said:

"Tell me what is in your mind. It cannot be all that difficult."

"I-it ... is difficult," the Princess said, "but ... I know I have to ... say it."

"I am listening."

"Lady Radstock," she began, so hesitantly that he could barely hear, "told me that the ... b-beautiful Lady Chatham was a ... very close ... friend of yours."

The Duke was surprised. This was certainly not what he had expected the Princess to say.

But he did not interrupt, and she went on:

"I think Lady Radstock meant that she was ... something more than a f-friend ... and as I know, from what I have read and heard, that men ... need a ... w-woman, I thought ... perhaps ... if I took her place ... it would prevent me from being so ... deeply in your ... d-debt."

The Duke was completely astounded.

Whatever he had expected the Princess to say to him, it was certainly not this.

And yet he could understand the way her mind had reasoned out that she had nothing to offer him except her own body.

Because he was English and because she disliked him, the sacrifice she was making to her own pride, in such a courageous manner, took his breath away.

For the moment he only stared at her, thinking
that he must have misunderstood what she had said.

Because he was silent, she looked up at him questioningly, and her eyes, dark and frightened, seemed
to fill her whole face.

"You are ... shocked ..." she said in the same low,
hesitating voice she had used before, "but I have ...
nothing else."

Nothing else, the Duke thought, except a beauty
which would stun most men and which was innocent,
untouched, and, as he was well aware, unawakened.

He thought that in these modern times, where in
their emancipation women had learnt all too quickly
about their own attractions and the easy way in which
they could obtain everything they desired, Militsa was
in fact unique.

She might have come from another planet or from
the moon itself into some alien world in which really
she had no part, because when it had moved from one
set of principles, morals, and ideals to another, she
had remained behind.

She was unchanged, beautiful, and as pure as one
of the Greek statues that he hoped Prince Ivan might
later find for him in Greece.

She was looking at him anxiously, her eyes searching his face, as if she could read in his expression his
reply to what she had offered.

As he too found it difficult to find words in which
to express himself, the Duke rose from his chair to
walk across the cabin to the port-hole.

Outside, the sea was still blue and the horizons
had already vanished in the mist since the sun had
gone down and it would soon be dark.

He had a strange feeling that he had stepped into
some mythical world which had nothing in common
with the life he had been living these last six years.

Then he remembered what had been said, and he
turned, knowing that Militsa was holding her breath
while she waited.

He deliberately spoke in the same indifferent
voice he had used before.

"I am, of course," he said, "prepared to tell you

that what you have suggested is quite unnecessary,
and I am more than willing to give both you and your
father anything you require without any strings attached."

Militsa made a little gesture with her hands and
it was the first time she had moved since she had sat
down, but she did not speak, and the Duke went on:

"Yet, because I understand your feelings and your
pride regarding being in my debt, of course I accept
your offer."

He thought she gave a little sigh, but whether
it was one of relief or despair he was not sure.

She was still for a moment, then she too rose to
her feet.

"You will . . . understand," she said, "that as I am
very . . . ignorant about such . . . things, I will not . . .
know what to . . . do."

The Duke felt that the last word came to her lips
with difficulty, and now she was no longer looking at
him but at the books on the wall beside him.

He had the feeling, however, that she was not
seeing them but reinforcing her own pride within
herself and forcing down her fears, trying instead to
be glad because she had got her own way and had
assuaged her own pride.

"I suggest," the Duke said, "that you leave everything in my hands. There is no need to be in a hurry,
as we have not only a considerable voyage in front of
us, but your father will doubtless be in Hospital for a
long time."

Militsa inclined her head, and he went on:

"For the moment I would like you to dine with
me tonight, because like all Englishmen I dislike dining alone."

"I . . . I will . . . do that."

Her voice was so low that he could barely hear it.

Then, almost as if she had reached the end of her
tether, she said:

"Could I . . . now please . . . go and see if Papa is
. . . awake?"

"Yes, of course," the Duke agreed, "and if he is

feeling well enough, please send Dawkins to find me and I will come and talk to him."

He opened the cabin door as he spoke.

She did not look at him as she passed him, but he knew with the instinct he had used before where she was concerned that she was vividly conscious of him and she was also afraid.

After he had shut the door behind her he sat down at his desk and stared across the cabin.

He was alone, but he could still feel the vibrations of fear that Militsa had left behind.

Chapter Seven

The Duke, leaning over the rail and watching the sun rise, was aware that the door onto the deck had opened and Militsa had come through it.

Without moving or turning his head, he saw out of the corner of his eye that she took a few steps towards the rail, then saw him.

She stood still and he knew she was debating in her mind whether to turn and walk away quickly in the opposite direction, supposing that he had not noticed her.

Then, as if she had told herself that not only would she be running away but he had a right to her presence if he required it, she walked towards him.

Still he did not move, and only when she stood beside him did he say in a quiet, normal tone:

"Good-morning, Militsa. You are up early!"

"Papa has had a bad night," she answered. "He fell asleep only a little while ago, after Dawkins had given him a very large dose of his special medicine."

The Duke was aware how worried she was, and he said consolingly:

"We will be in Monte Carlo in three days from now."

Militsa gave a little sigh. Then as if she somehow felt comforted by his reassurance, she leant against the rail as he was doing and looked out to sea.

She was standing farther from him than any other woman would have done, but the Duke knew that it was a positive step forward in their relationship that she remained with him at all.

Ever since they had left Cairo he had been playing a game which intrigued and enthralled him until he felt that every move he made, and hers in response, was being planned as if on a chess-board.

The first night when they had dined together he had known when she came into the Saloon before dinner how nervous and apprehensive she was.

She looked very lovely in a dress that was made in the same style and cheap material as the one she had worn in the morning.

This one was a pale pink in colour, with a pattern of small roses on it, and the Duke thought it gave her a young, fairy-like quality that she had not had before.

It also accentuated the translucent light of her skin, the strange shadows in her hair, and the mysterious darkness of her eyes.

Even though they had a depth which made them mysterious, they were still very expressive.

"I think, as this is the first night we have eaten together," the Duke said as she came across the Saloon towards him, "that you should have a glass of champagne. I have one ready for you."

He gave it into her hand as he spoke, and he wondered if she had ever drunk champagne before, having been too young to be allowed it in the days when it flowed like water in the extravagant, exotic Palaces in St. Petersburg.

However, Militsa made no comment but sipped a little of the champagne, and the Duke said:

"You may have wondered why I have not given your father champagne to drink, but I thought claret was a better tonic."

"He is very fond of claret," Militsa replied, "and I thought that was perhaps your reason for sending him such old and excellent vintages."

"I was sure he would appreciate them," the Duke said.

They entered the Dining-Saloon and he knew that Militsa appreciated the excellent dishes which the

Chef provided. At the same time, when she looked at him, the fear was still in her eyes.

He set himself out to talk to her about things which he knew would interest her, and by the time dinner was finished they had had several spirited arguments.

He was aware that he was talking to her as he might have talked to Harry or to any of his other men-friends, and he could never remember dining with a woman and enjoying a conversation that was so entirely impersonal and at the same time so intelligent.

Once during an argument Militsa made a little gesture with her hand as she said:

"You know so much on so many subjects that you make me ashamed of my ignorance. Please tell which books I should read so that next time we talk about something I can be a more able opponent."

"Is that what you want to be?"

He was aware that most women wished to agree with him because they thought that in that way they would ingratiate themselves into his affections.

"Papa has always said," Militsa answered, "that arguments clarify the mind and compel us to analyse our convictions, which we are often too lazy to do until we put them into words."

"That is an excellent analysis of what you have been making me do this evening," the Duke said.

"But you have so many opportunities for expressing in words what you believe."

The Duke raised his eye-brows, and she explained:

"You can speak in the House of Lords, and I am sure that you entertain many Statesmen and politicians, as Papa used to do before the Revolution."

She gave a little sigh. Then she said:

"If only I had been old enough then to listen to what was being said!"

"You will find plenty of men now who are only too willing to talk if you will listen to them," the Duke answered cynically.

"Perhaps I was foolish not to join you and your

friends when you asked me to," she said in a low voice.

The Duke realised that she was humbling herself in making what was, to all intents, an apology.

He told himself that if she had been at the meals in question she would have been disappointed.

Dolly always made quite certain that there was never a serious political or intellectual discussion when she was present. Instead they mostly laughed and capped one another's stories.

The discussion he had just had with Militsa was very different from anything which had been said in the Dining-Saloon on other nights.

They went on talking for a long time after the stewards had withdrawn, leaving the Duke with a glass of brandy at his side, which he preferred to port.

Then at last, almost reluctantly they left the Saloon, and now that there was no longer a table between them the Duke was aware that Militsa was once again uncertain of herself.

"I think Papa will be ... asleep," she said, "and perhaps I too ... should go to ... bed."

The words seemed almost to drag themselves from between her lips, and the Duke was aware that she was afraid of what would happen now.

"I think that is a good idea, Militsa," he replied. "It has been a long day with a lot of worries and you must be tired."

He realised that she was looking at him questioningly, and after a moment he added:

"I hope tomorrow morning you will breakfast with me at about eight-thirty, if that is not too early?"

He saw by the expression in her eyes that she understood the message he was giving her.

"I shall be awake much ... earlier than ... that," she said in a voice in which there was a little tremor. "Good-night ... Your Grace!"

"Good-night, Militsa!" the Duke replied gravely.

*   *   *

The following evening he knew as they sat down to dinner that she was eager to begin to talk about his

visit to India, and he was sure that she had been con-
sidering during the day on what subject she could
"pick his brains."

The questions she asked him were sometimes unanswerable, but once again the Duke found that he
was enjoying talking to her.

He also found it extremely flattering to be listened
to as if he were the source of all wisdom, a compliment
which neither Dolly nor any of his other loves had ever
conferred on him.

When at last the time came to say good-night, he
was sure Militsa was wondering what he might do and
telling herself that whatever it was, she was obliged to
obey him.

He conducted her along the passage to her cabin
but once again he said good-night without attempting
to touch her and made her aware that he would not
see her again until the following day.

Now as she leant over the rail near him, the Duke
felt that she was like a wild animal who was beginning
to trust him and yet was still wary and easily frightened.

"It is so beautiful!" Militsa said almost as if she
spoke to herself.

She was watching the sun disperse the morning
mist which lay over the sea.

"I have always believed that Russians feel beauty
and are more sensitive in other respects than other
people," the Duke replied.

"That may be true," Militsa said, "but when we
were so afraid and so hungry, it was very difficult to
forget the physical and reach out towards the spir-
itual."

The Duke thought with a little smile that few people could have put so simply what they had experienced.

He had known himself that in moments of danger
and when suffering from lack of water in the desert, it
had been almost impossible to think about anything
but what was actually happening.

"Now everything seems more . . . vivid, more . . .

wonderful than it has ever done before," Militsa was
saying.

"That is what I want you to feel," the Duke answered, "and it is easier to appreciate beauty when
there are not a lot of people to distract one's mind."

He was thinking of Dolly as he spoke and how
she saw beauty in nothing but jewels and therefore
prevented him when, he was with her, from appreciating many things that would otherwise have interested
him.

He had a sudden wish that he could be with
Prince Ivan, searching for the treasures of the past in
the Valley of the Kings at Luxor, and he thought that
when his present task of bringing the Grand Duke
back to health was over, he would return to Egypt,
but this time without Dolly.

Almost as if she could read his thoughts, Militsa
said:

"I am sure if we had not hurried you away in such
an ... inconvenient manner, you would have found not
only ... beauty but also ... the treasures you wished
for in Egypt."

"Prince Ivan will do that for me."

"But it will not be the same as finding them ...
yourself."

"There is plenty of time for that in the future,"
the Duke replied. "Now I have to look after your father and you, and that is more important than the
long-dead past."

"I do not wish to feel that we are the ... encum-
brances that we ... undoubtedly are," Militsa said.

"I think you are being hyper-sensitive about your
present position in my life," the Duke replied. "Perhaps I should tell you that I am a very selfish person,
and if I had really wished to go treasure-hunting with
the Prince, I would have arranged for you and your
father to go to Monte Carlo without me."

He saw that this idea had not struck her, and for
the first time since she had joined him she turned her
head to look at him.

"Why did you not do that?"

"Because I wanted to make sure that your father's operation was successful. Moreover, I can say in all sincerity that I am enjoying every moment of this trip, and especially our conversations."

"Do you really . . . mean that?"

"I always say what I mean."

"You know that I enjoy them too, because you tell me so much I want to learn."

"Then there is no need for either of us to make apologies to the other. We are both doing what we want to do."

"Yes . . . that is . . . true."

As if again she felt a little shy, she turned away to look out at the sea.

Now the mist had vanished before the warmth of the sun and the Duke felt it was an omen.

After they had eaten breakfast he spent some time with the Grand Duke, and he had the feeling that the old man was weaker.

He also learnt from Dawkins that the bouts of pain were more severe and more frequent.

Because he thought it was a mistake to talk of this to Militsa, the Duke concentrated on interesting her with his tales of different lands, the political situation in Europe, and the way England after the crises of war was gradually moving towards a somewhat precarious prosperity.

"There is still a vast amount of unemployment," he said, and saw by the expression on Militsa's face that she thought in that case it would be difficult for her to find herself a job.

He knew that sooner or later he would explain to her that the type of life he intended for her was very different from a struggle to make a living in what was still a male-dominated society.

But he felt that this was not the moment, and therefore he changed the subject to something that did not concern her personally.

That night after Militsa had left him rather later than usual to go to bed, he had sat thinking for a long time in his private cabin.

He had intended to read and had actually brought

several books from their shelves to look up dates of various subjects that he intended to discuss the following day.

Instead, he found himself thinking about her until, at one o'clock in the morning, he decided he should go to bed.

He was walking towards his cabin when he heard a door open and saw Militsa come out of her father's cabin and stare about her wildly as if she was seeking help.

The Duke hurried towards her.

She put out her hand to hold on to him as he reached her.

"Papa!" she exclaimed. "I think he is having some sort of . . . seizure, and I do not . . . know what to . . . do!"

The Duke moved quickly past her into the cabin.

One look at the Grand Duke told him that Militsa was right, and the old man was gasping for breath.

The Duke lifted him higher on his pillows and said sharply:

"Brandy and a spoon!"

Militsa brought them to him and he gave the Grand Duke a few drops of brandy. After a moment the colour came back to his face and he began to breathe more easily.

The Duke made him as comfortable as he could, then sat down beside him, taking his pulse as he did so.

The Grand Duke's hand was very cold and his pulse was so faint that the Duke found it hard to locate.

Militsa was watching him from the other side of the bed.

"He should have a Doctor," she whispered.

The Duke had the feeling that no Doctor, however experienced, would be able to do anything for the Grand Duke now, and at that moment he opened his eyes.

It was obviously difficult for him to focus on anything, and Militsa moved a little nearer to him to say:

"Are you all right, Papa?"

It took the old man a second or so to realise that she was there. Then as if he recognised her he said.

"Militsa!"

"I am here, Papa, and so is the Duke. We are worried about you."

With what seemed an effort the Grand Duke looked at the man whose hand was on his wrist. Then he said slowly and faintly:

"Look—after—Militsa."

Then as he said the last words his eyes closed, his head fell sideways onto his shoulder, and the Duke could no longer feel his pulse.

He knew what had happened, but Militsa stared at her father wildly, then went to the bedside with the bottle of brandy from which the Duke had filled the spoon.

"Give him some more brandy—quickly!" she cried.

The Duke rose and put the Grand Duke's hand gently down on his chest, then turned to say to her:

"There is nothing more we can do."

It seemed as if for a few seconds Militsa did not understand. Then with an inarticulate little murmur she moved as if instinctively towards the Duke and hid her face against his shoulder.

He put his arms round her and as he did so was aware that she was wearing nothing but a thin nightgown that she had borrowed from Nancy.

Her hair streaming over her shoulders reached to her waist, but since entering the cabin he had been too preoccupied to think of anything but the Grand Duke.

Now, holding Militsa against him, he knew that he wanted to protect and look after her, and he felt differently about her from the way he had felt about any other woman before.

He could feel her trembling against him. She was not crying, only fighting for control, feeling as if her whole world had collapsed about her and she was conscious not of herself but of the ruins of it.

"It is hard to think of it now," the Duke said very gently, "but your father has been saved a lot of pain.

In fact it is doubtful if the operation, if it had taken place, would have been successful."

"I cannot ... believe he has ... left me," Militsa said in a voice that was hard to hear and which broke on the last words.

"He is at peace," the Duke said.

He took Militsa to her own cabin and sent for Dawkins.

"I was afraid this would happen, Your Grace," Dawkins said. "His Royal Highness was getting weaker and weaker every day."

"I thought that too," the Duke agreed.

"Do you intend to have him buried at sea, Your Grace?"

"That is a good idea, Dawkins."

He went from the Grand Duke's cabin to Militsa's.

She was lying on her bed as he had left her, and as he expected she was not asleep but staring wide-eyed in front of her as if she was looking into the unseen.

She did not seem either embarrassed or surprised when he came to her, and he had the feeling that she was numb with shock and could think of nothing but her father.

He sat down beside the bed and took her hand in his.

"I want you to listen to me, Militsa," he said, "and it is important."

Her fingers tightened on his, but he knew it was an entirely impersonal reaction since for the moment he stood for the only thing that was secure and stable in her life.

"I have been thinking," he said, "that it would be a mistake to let the Bolsheviks be aware that your father is dead as they wished him to be. Let them go on worrying as to whether he is alive or not, and I think for your own point of view it would be easier for you not to have to answer questions about your escape from Russia."

"I ... think I ... understand," Militsa said after a moment's hesitation, "and I have no wish to ... talk about ... Papa to strangers."

"Of course not," the Duke agreed. "That is why I am asking whether you would like him to be buried at sea. That way, there would be no enquiries, no gloomy Churchyard Service, and above all no publicity."

"I would, of course, hate all that!" Militsa replied.

"Then, if I have your permission," the Duke continued, "I will bury His Royal Highness tomorrow morning at dawn."

It was impossible for her to speak, and the Duke rose.

Her hand was still in his and he raised it to his lips.

"You are very brave," he said quietly, and went from the cabin.

*   *   *

The following day, as the sun rose over the horizon, the Grand Duke was committed to the deep.

The Duke thought it had been a very moving ceremony, in which the Captain had read the Burial Service before the Grand Duke's body was lowered gently into the sea.

To the Duke's surprise, Militsa joined him at luncheon, and although she was very pale he had the feeling that she had not cried, and he remembered when he looked at her the line that followed the words that occurred to him so often.

> *And burning Pride and high Disdain*
> *Forbade the rising tear to flow.*

Could pride be more effective, he asked himself, than in checking the tears which would have brought any other woman to a state of hysteria?

He was filled with admiration when during luncheon she talked naturally of her father, describing what he had meant to her when she was a child and how even in the worst days of their years in hiding she had been happy and in a way content because she was with him.

Once or twice her voice trembled when she spoke of the old days, but the Duke thought her over-all courage and perhaps her pride gave her a new beauty.

Only after luncheon, when usually she had left him to go to her father, did she seem somehow at a loss.

Perceptively the Duke was aware that if she went below she would be acutely conscious of the empty cabin next to hers.

"I am going on the bridge," he said. "Why do you not join me? I would like you to see how we navigate *The Siren*."

"I would like to do that," Militsa answered.

"I think you ought to take a coat with you," the Duke said. "It seems warm at the moment, but the wind in the Mediterranean at this time of the year can be very treacherous, and it would be wise to bring it."

Because he saw that she hesitated, he sent a steward to her cabin to fetch it for her.

He carried it over his arm and they walked along the deck to the bridge.

He thought how slim and frail she looked. Life seemed to have dealt her blow after blow, yet while most women would have been bemoaning their fate and trying to evoke sympathy, she was behaving in a manner which he wondered if, in similar circumstances, he would have found possible.

She found the navigating of the ship extremely interesting, as he had thought she would, and afterwards he took her down to see the engines.

He wondered when she left him whether she would make some excuse not to dine with him, but she said nothing.

When he went to his private cabin he found that after being awake most of the night, his head began to nod and he slept until it was time to dress for dinner.

Only when he was waiting for Militsa in the Saloon did Dawkins appear instead to say:

"Her Serene Highness is fast asleep, Your Grace, and I think it would be a mistake to wake her."

"Yes, of course," the Duke agreed. "Let her sleep. It is the best thing for her."

The next day Militsa was very apologetic.

"I am sorry I left you to dine alone," she said, "which you told me you did not like."

"It was entirely understandable in the circumstances," the Duke replied. "You were very tired."

"I slept until Dawkins woke me this morning to bring me my early-morning tea."

The Duke told her how he too had fallen asleep in his cabin before dinner, and she gave a little laugh.

"Why are you laughing?" he enquired.

"It is almost incredible to find that you have human frailties. You always seem to me to be so strong, almost omnipotent, that I cannot believe you ever have a cold or bleed if you prick your finger."

The Duke laughed and realised that it was the first time Militsa had talked to him so lightly.

When they had finished breakfast he said:

"I want to ask you something."

"What is it?" she enquired.

"Nothing frightening," he said. "I only want to know if you would mind if we proceed to Monte Carlo as we had intended."

"Is that where you wish to go?"

"I sent instructions to open my Villa, but if you prefer we can change our plans and remain on the yacht."

Militsa was searching his face.

"Which do you want to do?" she enquired.

"I will be honest and say that I would like to go to Monte Carlo, if only for a day or so."

"Then of course I agree to that."

"Very well. We should be there tomorrow morning, and thank you for being so amenable."

"I did not know I had ever been anything else."

"I can answer that quite easily," the Duke said. "You are a woman, and all women are unpredictable."

There was a faint smile on Militsa's lips as she said:

"You forget that these last six years I have been with three men who have taught me, if nothing else, not to be a nuisance!"

"That is certainly reassuring."

That evening after dinner as they went to the Saloon the Duke said:

"This is our last night on board and I shall miss the quiet dinners we have had together. I was glad we were alone rather than surrounded by other guests."

"I too was . . . glad."

Thinking that perhaps she had been over-effusive, a faint colour came into her cheeks.

The Duke did not speak, and after a moment's silence she said:

"Were you going to talk to me about the . . . future?"

"I thought there was no need, unless you feel your debt can be cancelled now that I have not to pay for your father's operation."

"I still . . . owe you for what you have done for him and me . . . up until now," Militsa said in a low voice, "and if you do not . . . want me . . . I am afraid I shall have to . . . borrow a little money from you, in order to live until I . . . can . . . find work."

"Then our agreement still stands."

His eyes met hers as he spoke, and for a moment they looked at each other.

Then, because she was shy, with an effort she broke the spell between them by turning away.

"I . . . think I should . . . go to bed."

"That is a good idea," the Duke agreed, "and you should not tire yourself by reading until the early hours."

"How did you know I do that?"

"Shall I say I have noticed the number of books that have been removed from their places, and which come back phenomenally quickly."

"That is how I know what to ask you about, and unless you tell me, how can I learn?"

"The answer to that," the Duke said with a smile, "is that you are doing the right thing, but not tonight, Militsa. We have a great deal to do tomorrow, so that is an order!"

He knew she was curious, but she did not ask any questions.

She only moved away with a grace that he found once again reminded him of a small wild animal that has never known the restrictions of captivity.

They docked in Monte Carlo Harbour long before the pleasure-seekers were awake and perhaps even before the last gamblers had left the Casino.

The Duke's car which he kept there was waiting to carry them outside the town and up to the hills where his Villa was situated.

It was impressively spacious and had been built by his father in the last years of his life when his Doctors had ordered him to a warmer climate.

The late Duke had then spent a great deal of time and money in making the garden one of the most impressive sights in the Principality, and as Militsa stepped out of the car she gave an exclamation of delight.

The vivid beauty of the flowers contrasted with the dark, high-pointed cypress trees, and beyond them the wide vista of the sea was breath-taking.

"It is lovely!" she exclaimed. "Why did you not tell me? I did not imagine you owned such a beautiful place."

"I think that is somewhat of an obscure insult," the Duke replied drily.

He thought she glanced at him a little apprehensively in case he was angry. Then when she saw that he was smiling, she said:

"I think I was expecting your ... taste to be more ... conventional."

"What you are saying," the Duke replied, "is that I am English and therefore unimaginative and unable to appreciate beauty in the same way as you do."

"That is not true!" she protested.

He knew she was only being polite and that in fact that was what she had thought.

Inside the Villa, the valuable collection of paintings on the white walls and the exquisitely woven rugs on the polished floors were as lovely as the garden.

Militsa walked round the paintings, staring in delight, and the Duke knew this was another pleasure of which she had been starved.

"A Rubens!" she exclaimed. "Papa used to talk to me about his paintings. He tried to make me remember what they were like, but I found it difficult to recall all we had in our Palace in St. Petersburg."

"There are other rooms in the Villa in which you will find plenty to admire," the Duke said, "but when we have had breakfast you will have a very different matter requiring your attention."

"What is . . . that?"

"I ordered by telegram a large number of clothes to be ready for you on your arrival. Even so, when the dressmaker brings them, I expect you will find there are various alterations to be made."

Militsa looked at him as if it was the last thing she had expected, and he knew that for one moment she was about to say that she could not accept them from him.

Then, reading her thoughts, he knew that she remembered her position and told herself that a mistress accepted what the man to whom she had given herself wished to give her.

The Duke suspected that she had learnt from Nancy that Dolly had a penchant for jewellery and that that was what she was searching for in Constantinople.

Militsa was too quick-witted not to be aware that because she was now, as Nancy had put it, a "very close friend" of the Duke's, he would pay for whatever jewellery was bought when they were together.

He could almost see the way the thoughts were running through her mind. Then, as if she forced herself to be subservient, she said:

"Thank . . . you."

"You can thank me when you look beautiful as I want you to be," the Duke said.

He saw that she looked startled and added:

"I appreciate beauty in the same way you do, and, just as a painting requires the right sort of frame, so a beautiful woman should have the right clothes."

He saw that Militsa was thinking over what he had said, and she was silent until a man-servant came to the Duke's side to say in French:

"*Madame* Bertin has arrived, *Monsieur le Duc.*
She says she has an appointment."

"That is correct," the Duke said. "Show *Madame*
Bertin up to Her Serene Highness's bedroom."

The servant bowed, and when he left the room
Militsa asked:

"How ... many gowns may I ... buy?"

"That is all arranged," the Duke replied. "I have
given *Madame* Bertin my orders, but if there is anything you do not like, you must say so. When you have
finished with her, send *Madame* down to me."

Militsa looked at him indecisively and after a moment he said:

"Hurry! Otherwise the clothes which are waiting
for you may prove merely figments of your imagina-
tion and fly out the window! Then you will be left in
the most fashion-conscious place in the whole world
with nothing to wear except what you have on!"

As he spoke, he thought there was no woman who
could resist this, and with an exclamation that was half
a cry and half a laugh, Militsa left the room.

There was a smile on the Duke's lips as he walked
through the open window and out into the flower-filled
garden.

*   *   *

It was several hours later, after *Madame* Bertin
had gone, that Militsa came shyly across the lawn to
where the Duke was sitting comfortably in the shade,
reading a newspaper.

He knew as she walked towards him in an expensive gown of pale blue chiffon that she was acutely
conscious that she not only looked different but felt
different.

As she reached him she looked at him with an
expression in her eyes which he had never seen before
and said:

"How can I ... thank you for all the ... wonderful
clothes and everything else ... the stockings ... the
shoes ... the nightgowns? I did not even know such
lovely things existed."

"You will soon get used to them," the Duke said,

"and I am sure that like all women you will tell me you have nothing to wear!"

Militsa laughed a little uncertainly. Then she said:

"It will take... years to wear ... everything I have ... already."

She spoke without thinking.

Then she glanced at the Duke as if she asked him silently how long she was to stay with him and whether it would be weeks or even days before he told her she had paid her debt and he had no more use for her.

In the afternoon he took her driving, and while she found Monte Carlo entrancing and the views breath-taking, the Duke was thinking that in the white hat, shoes, gloves, and sunshade she looked beautiful.

She would be, he was certain, the envy of the women who in the Villas and Restaurants were already discussing his arrival.

The Siren in the harbour would have proclaimed his presence long before the newspapers wrote about him.

However, if anybody came to call, he and Militsa were not aware of it.

He had instructed the servants to say he was not at home, and as dusk fell with the swiftness of the time of year and turned to darkness, the Duke said:

"I am taking you out after dinner this evening, and I want you to wear for the occasion a special gown which *Madame* Bertin told me she brought with her this morning."

"There was one very lovely one," Militsa replied. "She said it was a Ball-gown, but I could not help wondering whether I would ever wear it."

"I promise you will attend quite a number of them."

He did not wait for her to ask questions but went on:

"Go and rest, and wear that particular gown to-night, because it will please me."

She went upstairs and he did not see her again until she came down dressed for dinner.

The gown was very different from the other evening-dresses *Madame* had brought with her.

For one thing, it was a picture-gown and the hem touched the ground. It was white, embroidered with silver diamanté which shimmered in the light.

To Militsa it was a fairy-creation that she thought her mother might have worn at one of the great Balls at the Winter Palace.

She thought when she was dressed that perhaps that was what the Duke had in mind when he had ordered it.

She was sure there was not only approval but also a glint of admiration in his eyes when he looked at her, but he only said:

"You look charming! Dinner is ready. Shall we go in?"

The Chef in the Villa was, if possible, even better than the one on board *The Siren*.

Soon they were engaged in one of their fascinating arguments, which made Militsa feel as if she fenced with the Duke and had to parry every thrust he made.

Yet, because he was so much cleverer than she was, invariably he broke through her guard.

When dinner was over, the competent French maid who had helped Militsa dress was waiting in the Hall with a velvet wrap edged with white fox and a lace scarf to cover her head.

It was of exquisitely fine lace and so long that it reached over her shoulders to touch the hem of her gown.

Knowing that the night was cold, she felt that the Duke was preventing her as he had aboard from feeling the chill.

A car was waiting and they drove downhill towards the sea.

The Duke was rather silent after they had been talking so animatedly during dinner and Militsa wondered what he was thinking.

'He is so kind ... and I want to ... thank him, even though he does not wish me to,' she thought.

The car came to a standstill and she realised they were outside a house. Then to her surprise she saw that there were only a few lights in some of the windows.

"This Villa belongs to a Russian who escaped the Revolution," the Duke said. "He is not here at the moment, but I have something to show you."

He helped her out of the car and they entered a Hall which was filled with the fragrance of flowers. A servant took Militsa's wrap but the veil remained.

The Duke drew her along the passage and as they reached the end of it there was the sound of music.

It was soft and deep and seemed, Militsa thought, like the notes of an organ. She was immediately apprehensive in case there were people waiting for them.

The Duke had given her his arm, and now as her fingers tightened on his, she said:

"I . . . I shall not know . . . how to . . . behave."

The Duke stopped.

"It is not a party," he answered. "It is in fact a Private Chapel of the Russian Orthodox Church, to which I know you belong."

He saw the astonishment in her eyes. Then he said:

"Your father told me to look after you, and that is what I intend to do—as my wife!"

Militsa was absolutely still.

Then he knew that both her hands were holding on to him as if she were afraid she might fall.

"Y-you are . . . asking me to . . . m-marry you?" she asked in a voice he could barely hear.

He shook his head.

"I am not asking you—I am commanding you!" he said. "In the same way as you demanded my help, and it is just as impossible for you to refuse."

He looked into her eyes as he spoke, and Militsa knew that he meant what he said and there was nothing she could do but obey his command.

He understood what she was feeling although she could not put it into words.

Then he drew her forward through an open door

into the light of the candles on the altar and those
flickering in silver sanctuary lamps hanging from the
arched roof.

*			*			*

Driving back towards the Villa, Militsa felt as if
she were in a dream from which it was impossible to
awaken.

The Service, the prayers that were said before the
sacred Ikons, the lighted candles that she and the
Duke held, and the crowns that were held over their
heads made a pattern of beauty that she knew she
would never forget.

It would always be there in her heart.

As the Duke had made his responses in a deep
voice and she had heard her own replies, shy and a
little tremulous, she had felt her whole being vibrate
to strange music, not of the organ, but which came
from a paean of joy rising within her very soul.

She felt herself carried away by a rapture which
seemed to intensify from the moment the Duke put
the ring on her finger and they knelt for the blessing.

Now she was alone with the man who was her
husband—the man whom she had hated but for whom
she now felt a very different emotion—one that was
difficult to express even to herself.

They reached the Villa and as they stepped out
of the car the Duke said:

"There is some champagne upstairs in your Sit-
ting-Room with which to drink to our future."

Militsa had had a brief glimpse of the *Boudoir*
which opened off her bedroom.

She was aware that it was beautiful like the rest
of the Villa, and now as she and the Duke entered
it, she found that it had been decorated with white
flowers, and with the lights turned down low, it
had a fairy-like loveliness which made it seem as un-
real as the whole evening had been.

Instinctively she stood looking about her, and
felt the Duke take her fur-lined wrap from her shoulders.

He then removed the veil she had worn over her hair, and she thought she had been very foolish not to recognise that it was a wedding-veil.

She looked at the Duke and saw that there was a faint smile on his lips and an expression in his eyes that she had never seen before.

The question that was uppermost in her mind came impulsively to her lips.

"How can you have ... wanted to ... marry me?"

"I knew when your father died and you turned to me for comfort," the Duke replied, "that I had to look after you, not in the way you had offered but for the rest of our lives."

"Is that ... what you ... want?" Militsa questioned.

"I think I can tell you more eloquently what I want without words."

He moved towards her as he spoke.

Then as his arms went round her, he felt her quiver as she hid her face against his shoulder.

"This is how I held you before," he said quietly, "and I knew then that I had fallen in love."

What he said was so surprising that Militsa raised her eyes to look up at him, and as she did so, she found that his lips were very close to hers.

For one long moment the Duke looked at her. Then his mouth came down on hers and held her captive.

For a moment he was conscious only that her lips were very soft, innocent, and unsure. Then as his kiss deepened and he held her closer, he knew that for him this kiss was different from any other kiss he had ever known.

As he felt Militsa quiver, he was aware that just as he was feeling the wonder of it, so was she.

He knew he had found something for which he had always sought and which had eluded him until now, and it was even more wonderful and glorious than he had imagined it could ever be.

He felt Militsa respond to him in a way he had not expected.

He had thought that because she was so young, innocent, and inexperienced, it would take him a long time to awaken her to the wonder of love.

He had been prepared to wait, to control himself as he had these last days during their time on the yacht.

But he had not expected that every day, every hour, and indeed every moment he was with her, he was loving her more and desiring her as he had never desired a woman before in his whole life.

As his kiss became more demanding, more possessive and insistent, he found that there was in fact a fire beneath the pride that was so much a part of Militsa that he could hardly imagine her without it.

And yet love was making her burn with a very different emotion and one which he knew would be strengthened until it became the flaming furnace that he himself felt burning consumingly through him.

Because he wanted to be gentle and tender and not to spoil the fragile beauty that was spiritually so much a part of her, he raised his head to say in a voice that was curiously unsteady:

"Now tell me what you feel about me."

There was a faint flush on her cheeks, her lips were red from his kisses, and her eyes held a light that had never been there before.

"I hated ... you," she said at last, "but now I ... know it was from the very ... beginning a ... part of my ... love."

"From the beginning?" the Duke questioned.

"When I first ... saw you in your cabin, you ... frightened me."

She thought the Duke did not understand, and she explained quickly:

"Not only because I was afraid you would not do what we asked, but because you were so ... handsome, so overwhelming, so commanding! It was what I had always believed a man should be ... like, and yet because you had so much while we had so little, I told myself I ... hated you."

The Duke's arms tightened round her and he merely said:

"Go on. Then what happened?"

"Papa and the others had all been quite certain you would not do what we asked, and because I was afraid you might refuse, I hated you for that. Then when you took us on the yacht, I hated the contrast between your wealth and our poverty."

"I can understand that," the Duke said. "I saw you look at me with hatred in your eyes."

"I hated you for what you made me feel," Militsa said, "and that is why I did not wish to see you, or talk to you, or go near you."

"Then what did you feel?" he asked.

"Very strange feelings, almost as if my heart was calling . . . to yours, and that . . . something within me . . . reached out to something that . . . came from . . . you."

"Vibrations!" the Duke exclaimed. "I felt them. I felt them from the first moment you came to the yacht, and when we drove together in that ramshackle vehicle to the empty house."

"And when we . . . were on the . . . yacht," Militsa said, "some part of me belonged to you . . . and yet I went on . . . fighting it, because I was . . . jealous."

She whispered the last words and turned to hide her face against his neck.

He kissed her hair before he said:

"I had no idea you felt like that. I only knew that after I had seen you, no other woman attracted me."

He felt her quiver against him. Then as if she had to know that that was true, she lifted her face to look at him.

"Did . . . you really feel like . . . that?"

"I promise you that is the truth," he said, "but like you I fought against the strange feelings which I found difficult to understand. But it was no use: there was only one woman in the whole world, and that was you!"

Militsa began to give a little cry of delight, but the Duke stopped it because he was kissing her, kissing her with fierce, demanding kisses, as if he would force her love from her lips.

Even as he did so, he knew that just as he had given her his heart irretrievably and forever, so he had taken hers into his keeping, and she was his completely and absolutely....

When they were both breathless, he said hoarsely:

"Get into bed, my precious. I want to be closer to you than I am at the moment."

He kissed her again and went quickly into his bedroom on the other side of the *Boudoir* as if he had to force himself to leave.

As he took off his white tie, tail-coat, and stiff shirt, he thought he was so thrilled, happy, and excited that he was like a young boy with his first love.

He did not take long, and when he went back he was wearing a blue silk dressing-gown with his monogram surmounted by a coronet on the breast-pocket.

He looked very handsome as he opened the door of Militsa's bedroom. Fragrant with flowers, with a light only by the big white-canopied bed, it was very romantic.

But to his surprise Militsa, still dressed, was standing in the centre of the room.

He felt that something was wrong.

"What is it? What thas happened?" he asked.

"I cannot ... undo my ... gown," she answered in a helpless little voice. "You will ... think I am very ... stupid."

The Duke smiled as he walked towards her.

"My darling, forgive me. I should have remembered you have not had complicated gowns to cope with these last years."

She looked at him almost as if she was afraid he was angry with her. Then when she saw the tenderness in his eyes, she threw herself against him and burst into tears.

He held her closely.

"My precious love! My sweet! You must not cry. You have been so wonderfully brave, I cannot bear you to be unhappy."

"I am not ... unhappy," she sobbed. "I am happy ... so wildly ... happy ... that I can't ... believe it."

"It is true, my lovely darling."

"I was so . . . afraid when Papa . . . died," she whispered incoherently, "and I was all . . . alone . . . I don't want to earn . . . my living . . . I don't want to be proud but . . . safe with . . . you."

"Which you are and always will be," the Duke answered, with his lips against her hair.

"You are . . . sure . . . really sure you love . . . me?"

"Very, very sure," he said. "But you must not cry, my love."

As he spoke, he thought that it was the breaking-point of the barriers which she had erected between herself and the world as a kind of armour.

Now she was no longer proud, but his.

He put his fingers under her chin and lifted her face up. With the tears on her dark lashes and on her cheeks, she looked so lovely that he stared at her as if he had never seen her before.

"I love you! I love you!" he said. "How can this have happened to us? Out of the whole world, how could I have been so fortunate as to find you?"

"That is . . . what I am saying," Militsa murmured. "I had no idea you would . . . love me. When I . . . offered you . . . myself, I pretended it was for no other reason than I must pay a debt of . . . gratitude, but I knew that if I could be with you if only for a . . . little while, it would be . . . something to remember . . . for the . . . rest of my life."

"The rest of your life will be spent with me," the Duke said firmly, "and, my darling, I know we shall be ecstatically happy, even though I have had to fight a major battle against a very formidable enemy called 'Pride.' "

"I will never, never be . . . proud in the future," Militsa said humbly.

The Duke laughed.

"I assure you it is something I would not prevent or alter, and I shall be exceedingly proud of you, my beautiful darling."

"Do you . . . really think I am . . . beautiful?"

"I will convince you that you are very beautiful," the Duke answered, "but it is going to take a very long time."

"I will love that as I love talking to you!"

"I too enjoy talking to you," the Duke replied, "but now, my adorable wife, I have a lot to teach you about love."

He felt Militsa draw in her breath. Then she said in a voice that had a sudden note of passion in it:

"Teach me . . . please . . . teach me! I not only want to love you . . . but to make you . . . love me . . . and I am so . . . ignorant that I do not know . . . how to . . . begin."

"This is how we begin," the Duke said with his lips very close to hers.

He kissed her until the breath was coming quickly from between her lips, and then as he kissed her neck he knew that she vibrated with a dozen strange emotions which she had never known existed.

She was so alluring and so exciting that he himself was aroused by her physically and spiritually as he had never been before.

"I love you!" he exclaimed. "God, how I love you, my darling one! And I will be very gentle. I will not hurt or frighten you."

"I am . . . not frightened," she whispered. "I only . . . love you . . . until there is . . . nothing in the . . . world but . . . you."

Then as his lips held her captive and her body was invaded with a strange fire which burned away pride and hatred and everything except love, she felt him undoing the back of her gown.

ABOUT THE AUTHOR

BARBARA CARTLAND, the world's most famous romantic novelist, who is also an historian, playwright, lecturer, political speaker and television personality, has now written over 200 books.

She has also had many historical works published and has written four autobiographies as well as the biographies of her mother and that of her brother Ronald Cartland, who was the first Member of Parliament to be killed in the last war. This book has a preface by Sir Winston Churchill.

Barbara Cartland has sold 100 million books over the world, more than half of these in the U.S.A. She broke the world record in 1975 by writing twenty books, and her own record in 1976 with twenty-one. In addition, her album of love songs has just been published, sung with the Royal Philharmonic Orchestra.

In private life, Barbara Cartland, who is a Dame of the Order of St. John of Jerusalem, has fought for better conditions and salaries for Midwives and Nurses. As President of the Royal College of Midwives (Hertfordshire Branch), she has been invested with the first Badge of Office ever given in Great Britain which was subscribed to by the Midwives themselves. She has also championed the cause for old people and founded the first Romany Gypsy Camp in the world.

Barbara Cartland is deeply interested in Vitamin Therapy and is President of the British National Association for Health.

Bantam Book Catalog

Here's your up-to-the-minute listing of over 1,400 titles by your favorite authors.

This illustrated, large format catalog gives a description of each title. For your convenience, it is divided into categories in fiction and non-fiction—gothics, science fiction, westerns, mysteries, cookbooks, mysticism and occult, biographies, history, family living, health, psychology, art.

So don't delay—take advantage of this special opportunity to increase your reading pleasure.

Just send us your name and address and 50¢ (to help defray postage and handling costs).